A man's figure was silhouetted against the screen door . .

Her blood turned to ice. "Rasmus!"

Lantern light flickered grotesquely on the kitchen walls.

"Right the first time, Mrs. Knight. Rasmus Pierce, at yer service." His chuckle raised the hair on the back of her neck. "Or more precisely, yer at my service."

In the light from the battered lantern, his face was gray between his black derby and the thin beard that covered the bottom half of his face. His hair no longer curled over his collar, and the Vandyke beard had been sacrificed to an over-all beard.

Was he here to harm the children? *Stop that! Get your emotions under control,* Constance chided herself. *Don't let him know you're frightened. Remember your training.*

"What may I do for you, Mr. Pierce?"

"For starters, ya kin git inta the parlor, where we'll be more comfortable waitin' fer yer husband."

"My husband hasn't risen yet. Since you are so eager to speak with him, I'll waken him for you."

"Stop right there, Mrs. Knight."

She froze with her hand on the swinging door. Had that brushing sound been a gun being withdrawn from its holster? Why, why had she removed the pocket with her derringer earlier in the evening? She forced herself to turn about, swallowed her heart which had settled in her throat. Rasmus had a pistol leveled at her.

JOANN A. GROTE made her **Heartsong Presents** debut with the historical novel, *The Sure Promise*, a story set in western Minnesota where JoAnn was raised. Grote feels strongly that fiction has an important place in spreading God's message of salvation and encouraging Christians to become more like Christ.

Books by JoAnn A. Grote

HEARTSONG PRESENTS

HP36—The Sure Promise
HP51—The Unfolding Heart
HP55—Treasure of the Heart
HP103—Love's Shining Hope

Don't miss out on any of our super romances. Write to us at the following address for information on our newest releases and club information.

Heartsong Presents Readers' Service
P.O. Box 719
Uhrichsville, OH 44683

An Honest
Love

JoAnn A. Grote

Song of the River: Book One

Heartsong Presents

*Dedicated with love to
my brother (and banker)
J. Gary Olsen
and his wife
Helen*

A note from the Author:
*I love to hear from my readers! You may write to me at the
following address:*

JoAnn A. Grote
Author Relations
P.O. Box 719
Uhrichsville, OH 44683

ISBN 1-55748-703-0

AN HONEST LOVE

one

Constance Ward swayed against the purple plush seat, no longer noticing the rocking of the day car or the loud clacking of wheels against steel rails after eleven hours of travel.

Pinkerton's National Detective Agency hadn't given her an assignment outside Chicago since 1891, two years ago, and her gaze eagerly drank in the beauty of the countryside along the Mississippi River bordering southern Wisconsin and Minnesota.

The trip seemed more a vacation than an assignment. All that was required of her was to deliver her niece and nephew to her Aunt Libby in River's Edge, Minnesota, and become friendly with Mrs. Pierce. There was no danger involved. Mrs. Pierce's son, Rasmus, who had eluded law enforcement agencies for over five years, was reputed to be in Missouri.

A smile tugged at her lips as she watched Effie and Evan laughing with Justin Knight, the man across the aisle. The six-year-old twins looked so much like her brother, Charles, that the sight of them stung at the place in her heart that was still unhealed from his death six months earlier. Like Charles, the children had broad faces with snub noses, brown hair and huge brown eyes in contrast to her own pointed chin, green eyes and black hair, which she wore in a thick figure eight twist.

She'd been curious about the reserved Mr. Knight since he'd boarded at Chicago. When he revealed he was a banker from River's Edge, she'd found his presence even more intriguing. His acquaintance was fortuitous; she might be able to use it to advantage on her present case.

5

She'd thought Mr. Knight reserved until the first time he smiled at her. His chestnut brown eyes had flared with a sudden light that sent her heart tripping in a most unfamiliar manner. Then they warmed into an almost boyishly friendly glow.

Under the guise of watching the children scramble about him, she observed him as she would a suspect or so she tried to convince herself. He was about six inches taller than her five-foot-three frame, but his straight, broad shoulders and the assured manner in which he held his head made him appear taller. Brown hair parted on the side waved rebelliously just above his ears, refusing to be brought into submission.

Did his smile hint at a boyish spirit hidden inside the almost stern man that was just as difficult to tame as the waves in his hair? she wondered. Yet there was a quiet strength about him that instilled confidence. If her experiences as a Pinkerton investigator had taught her anything about judging character, this was a man who could be depended upon in life's storms.

She couldn't recall when she'd been so aware of a man, and a stranger at that! As the day wore on, he appeared to truly enjoy the twins' attention, and she found she was beginning to like this man to whom she'd been instantly and powerfully attracted.

It was through the children they finally exchanged greetings and unsatisfyingly small slices of information about themselves. Effie and Evan practically adopted the man, climbing about his perfectly tailored suit over Constance's protests, firing questions at him about himself and the areas through which they passed.

He looked up unexpectedly, catching her gaze on him, and a thrill danced along her nerves. With an effort, she shifted her glance to the few other passengers in the day car. Besides herself, the children and Mr. Knight, there were only four: two drummers who had boarded at the last station discussing hoped-for sales, a preacher dressed in black relieved only by the white collar at his throat, and across from him a man with a Vandyke beard and long black hair that curled against the back of his linen duster, sitting with his back to her in one of the first seats, his hat low over his forehead.

The man with the long hair rose and started toward them, adjusting his gait to the swaying of the car, just before Effie darted back across the aisle to fling herself eagerly against the black skirt of Constance's mourning gown. The child's exuberant actions unintentionally knocked Constance's alligator handbag to the floor with a thud, and it slid out of her reach beneath the opposite seat.

Effie smiled up at her with shining brown eyes, her hair flowing in shiny brown waves over the large cape collar of her blue and white striped dress. "Are we almost there, Aunt Constance?"

"Only a few more miles, dear."

Constance's answer was lost in the ice-cold voice of the long-haired stranger now leaning against the seat across the aisle.

"If it ain't Justin Knight, as I live and breathe."

Constance frowned. A warning in her brain which she'd come to respect during the last three years tugged at her. Now that she saw him up close, there was something familiar about the man's face.

"Rasmus." Mr. Knight's voice was tight as he acknowledged the man's sarcastic greeting.

A chill swept down her spine like a Chinook wind. Her hand's tightened on Effie's shoulders. *Rasmus!* Of course, Rasmus Pierce, the head of the very outlaw gang she'd been assigned to gather information on for the Pinkerton Agency! They'd thought he was in Missouri.

He looked nothing like the photo and description of him she carried in her handbag. She must inform the Superintendent in her next report that the gang leader had let his hair grow and was now sporting a beard and a narrow, almost slinky, black mustache.

She darted a glance to her handbag, still sliding around the floor. Her stomach churned. Her derringer was in that bag. Perhaps she was borrowing trouble, and wouldn't need the small firearm. The hope was dashed when the outlaw pushed aside his long linen duster to reach for a revolver.

A grin slithered across Rasmus' face as he pointed the barrel at Mr. Knight. He spat a wad of tobacco from the side of his mouth.

"I'd planned ta git rid of ya 'fore yer weddin' this Sunday, but circumstances bein' what they are, might be I've got another plan."

Constance noticed the slight widening of Mr. Knight's eyes in a face suddenly gone pale. His hand gripped Evan's shoulder, and Constance's heart caught in her throat at the fear that sat starkly on her nephew's wide face.

"Why not be a gentleman, and let the lady and these children move out of the way before dealing with me?" Mr. Knight's voice was stiff with barely controlled fury.

The outlaw ignored him. "Where's yer pa, boy?"

Evan trembled, unable to take his eyes from the gun barrel. Even the brown locks curling just below his ear lobes quivered. His mouth moved, but no words came out.

"I said, where's yer pa?"

"His father is dead." Constance was surprised her voice was so calm. She'd been in dangerous situations before, but never with Effie and Evan near. She had to keep her wits about her, as her fellow agent, Alexander Bixby, would say. It would take all she'd learned in her years as a detective to get them out of this unbelievable situation safely.

The slimy grin moved across the man's face again as he glanced at her. "Good." His gaze dropped quickly to her gloved hands and back to her face. "You his ma?"

"No."

"You a married lady?"

Why would he ask such a thing? She returned his look un-flinchingly. "No."

Effie pulled away from Constance's hands, plumped her hands on her hips and scowled at Rasmus.

"Why are you pointing that gun at my brother? You're a mean man!"

Fear spread fiery hot through her. She drew the girl back against her. "Shhh, dear. It's all right."

"He's mean! Tell him to stop being mean, Aunt Constance!"

Rasmus' eyes blazed. "Shut her up."

Dread thickened in her chest. She tried to keep her voice calm for the children's sake.

"Evan is fine. Mr. Knight is taking care of him. See?"

Mr. Knight smiled at Effie—a tight little smile, but a smile—and Constance could have hugged him. "That's right, Effie. Mr. Pierce is just playing games, as he and I used to do when we were boys."

Rasmus snorted. "Some game."

Mr. Knight jerked, and the gun lifted slightly. "Wouldn't try it, Knight. Wouldn't want a stray bullet hittin' one o' these kids, now, would we?"

His words threw a horrible picture across Constance's mind, sending terror racing through her. She pushed it away reso-lutely. There was nothing to be gained from imagining things.

Suddenly the train lurched, the wheels squealing along the rails, throwing the children heavily against Constance and Mr. Knight. Somehow Rasmus' henchmen must have managed to stop the train, Constance thought.

For the first time, she remembered the other passengers. Her gaze shot toward the men at the front of the car. Guns in hand, the "drummers" were standing either side of the door. One was watching the next car. The other had a gun trained on the pastor.

Mr. Knight's jaw clenched. "What is it you want?"

"Why, jest a weddin' thet's all. You and Marian fergot ta invite me ta yers." He nodded toward Constance. "Figure we have a lady here with no husband, a preacher ta do the tyin', and you jest itchin' ta git hitched. Might as well do the job right now. 'Sides, might not be safe fer me ta go ta a weddin' in town. Certain people wouldn't make me welcome."

Sweat trickled down Constance's back. Surely he wasn't suggesting—!

"Trying to get me out of the way so you can wed Marian yourself, Rasmus? She'll never have you."

Rasmus dumped the smile. The fire in his black eyes shot horror through Constance. What was Mr. Knight doing? Didn't he know Rasmus Pierce's reputation? The outlaw thought no more of shooting a person than he would a jackrabbit.

"Maybe Marian won't have me, Knight. But she'll hate you, humiliatin' her by marryin' someone else right before yer weddin's scheduled. And her hatin' you is almost as good as her marryin' me."

"Even you aren't so low you'd force a lady into a marriage with a stranger, Pierce."

Never had Constance heard such cold laughter as the outlaw's. "Wouldn't bet that new house of yers on it."

"No judge would uphold a marriage two strangers were forced into at the point of a gun." Constance thought she detected a hint of uncertainty in Mr. Knight's sarcasm.

Rasmus slouched lazily against the seat facing Mr. Knight. "But yer not goin' ta tell anyone this marriage warn't jest what ya wanted. See, if'n ya do, there's a couple kids might not git a chance ta grow up." His glittering eyes swept over Evan and Effie.

Constance's arms tightened around Effie. She searched Justin Knight's face. The children's lives were in his hands. What would he do?

His gaze met hers. Fear and anger had widened his pupils until blackness shoved away the warm brown of his eyes. He seemed to probe her very soul. What was he expecting to uncover? Would he find it?

The cocking of the revolver's hammer exploded through the car like a cannon blast. "Time's a-wastin'. What'll it be? A new bride and life, or. . ." He waved the pistol from Evan to Effie and back again.

Mr. Knight's gaze still bored into hers. "Miss Ward, will you do me the honor of becoming my wife?"

The detective in her admired his calm and command, even as she wondered how he could voice the question from a face as rigid as a statue's.

She remembered her first impression of him, a man to be depended upon in a storm, and a little of the fear clutching her heart released.

Lifting her chin, she squared her shoulders beneath leghorn sleeves. She could show a good deal of "spunk" herself, as the Superintendent had said more than once. Nodding slightly, she forced a bright smile. "I should be pleased to accept your proposal."

Rasmus' evil laughter filled the rail car. He swung his pistol in a gesturing motion and hollered, "Preacher, git yerself down here! Ya got a weddin' ta perform."

The reverend walked jerkily toward them, a worn leather Bible clutched in his hands, his lips moving silently. Was he praying for safety for himself, Constance wondered, or for them? He didn't look as if he had much faith in his God getting them out of the situation. He was trembling like the proverbial leaf, and his face was whiter than his collar.

"Sir, I beg of you, leave off harassing these people. The Lord. . ."

"Yer here ta perform a weddin', not give a sermon."

The reverend drew himself up taller. His trembling increased.

"I'll not be party to such doings."

Constance stared at him in surprise. So the man had courage after all, in spite of his obvious fear. But perhaps his courage was ill-timed. Rasmus Pierce was not a man with whom to trifle.

Pierce's eyes narrowed. His lips pulled back in a sneer over yellowed teeth. "P'raps ya didn't hear what will happen if there's no marriage." He glanced pointedly toward Evan, who by now was clutching Mr. Knight's hand until his little knuckles were white.

Mr. Knight's voice was steady. "We appreciate your efforts on our behalf, Reverend. However, they are unnecessary, as Miss Ward and I are willing participants in this ceremony. We'd be grateful for your services."

The preacher looked from Mr. Knight to Constance and back again.

"Very well." He ignored Rasmus Pierce in a manner which delighted Constance. Even such a little thing gave her the pleasurable thrill of revenge.

"Miss Ward, Mr. Knight, if you would be so good as to stand beside each other in the aisle, facing me, and take each other's hands, we will begin."

Constance rose, and Effie clutched at her hand, her brown eyes huge. "Are you truly going to marry him?"

She hoped her smile was reassuring. "Yes, dear. Would you and Evan do us the pleasure of being our wedding party?" Perhaps being part of this unreal ceremony would help calm them.

Effie glanced at Evan before nodding.

Mr. Knight squeezed Evan's hand. "What do you say, old man? It would mean a lot to me to have you stand up for me."

"Okay." The boy's reply was barely a whisper.

Constance smiled her gratitude at the man who would be her husband in a matter of minutes.

Amazing what little time it takes to change the course of a person's path for a lifetime, she thought as the ceremony ended. Of course, this wasn't a real marriage. They would have it annulled as soon as Rasmus was behind bars.

Unexpected pain compressed her heart. In spite of all the roles she'd played as an agent, she'd expected to play the role of bride only once. She felt tarnished from taking the vows with no intention of keeping them.

"Ain't ya goin' ta kiss yer bride?"

Constance felt the blood drain from her face. What a reprehensible man! She stood rigid as Mr. Knight touched cold lips to her cheek.

"Ya done real good, Preacher." Rasmus straightened from his slouch against the seat, his revolver still pointed at Evan. "Now, Mr. and Mrs. Knight, don't ya be fergettin' what I said 'bout these here younguns. I don't want Marion thinkin' this marriage was anyone's idea but yers. If'n I hear any rumors ta the contrary, I'll know where ta find these babes. I've got eyes and ears ever'where. Don't ferget it."

An explosion rocked the car, throwing Constance heavily against Mr. Knight, who fell against the window. Effie's scream was the only human sound in the car filled with thuds and clangs of people and objects banging together. The reverend grabbed for the upholstered arm of a seat, missed and landed on the floor. Only the bandits remained in control of themselves. They'd been braced against the seats or doors, Constance realized, as though expecting the explosion.

Screams from the car in front of them could still be heard as Constance and the others righted themselves.

"What was that?" Evan asked through pale lips.

"Rasmus' friends blew the safe in the express car, I expect." Rasmus raised his black eyebrows. "Good guess, Knight. In the other cars, my pals will be takin' up a collection from the passengers. But since you and the lady have been so cooperative, reckon we won't ask fer yer money and jewels."

Thank goodness! She hadn't much in the way of either, but if Rasmus discovered the card in her handbag identifying her as a Pinkerton agent, she'd be in grave danger.

Rasmus shot a glance out the window, then backed down the aisle. Grabbing his derby, he tipped it jauntily before settling it on his black hair.

"Time ta go. Be seein' ya 'round, newlyweds."

She wanted to smack the grin from his lean, slimy face, but stood quietly with her hands resting on Effie's shoulders, forcing her face to remain passive.

As soon as Rasmus and the "drummers" stepped from the car and dropped to the ground, she and Mr. Knight tore to the windows. A man with a bandanna over his face and a huge beige Stetson sat on a black horse, holding the reins of numerous other mounts. In a moment, the three outlaws were joined by others from the train, mounted and started off at a gallop.

The railroad men and passengers poured from the cars in front of them and ran toward the express car. Before Constance and Mr. Knight could follow, the reverend stopped them. She could see from his face that Mr. Knight was as impatient as she was herself at the distraction.

"I'm sorry you young people were forced into this marriage. But remember God's promise in the book of Romans: 'All things work together for good to them that love God.'"

"Thank you, Pastor," Constance murmured, and heard Mr. Knight thanking him also.

She turned to the children, admonishing them to stay where they were until she returned. Then she rushed down the aisle after Mr. Knight, one hand lifting the tailored skirt of her black traveling outfit, the other clutching her small, crepe-covered black mourning hat. Her superintendent would be expecting a report on the robbery. He would certainly not consider a wedding or a reverend adequate excuse for not discovering the details of the robbery herself.

The pastor's words swung in her mind as she ran. "All things work together for good."

What utter nonsense! This wedding would cause her endless complications. Doubtless it would eventually be annulled. But in the meantime, what would her Pinkerton superintendent say about the inconvenience caused to the investigation?

Religious people were generally tolerable, she'd found, since their Christian values kept them from involvement in too many crimes that hurt their fellow citizens. But they could be such fools, as the reverend's remark clearly showed.

two

It was an hour before the railroad officials had examined the situation, determined the extent of the loss and damage, and were satisfied no one had been harmed. The dynamite used to blow open the safe hadn't been strong enough to blow the roof off the baggage and express car, as Constance had seen happen on other occasions. But the blast did tear apart several boxes, trunks and valises, and their contents were scattered about the car.

Constance observed everything as closely as possible in the confusion, attempting to fill her memory with facts to include in her report at the earliest opportunity. It wasn't easy with her identity as a Pinkerton operative unknown. The railroad officials tried with little success to keep passengers distanced as they considered the situation. Twice Mr. Knight suggested she return to the children. Constance pretended not to hear him.

When the train finally shivered to a grunting, clanking start, Mr. Knight won Constance's gratitude by calming Effie and Evan, praising them richly, and telling them they had acted bravely and wisely.

Before long he diverted their thoughts by encouraging them to watch for the long bridge that would soon carry the train over the Mississippi into River's Edge. They moved across the aisle, taking up residence on their knees upon the amethyst upholstered couches, noses pressed eagerly against the windows. Early-turning russet and golden leaves occasionally brightened the green pine along the high, craggy bluffs bordering the river. Steamboats and barges dotted the water.

Towboats floated huge rafts of lumber from northern Minnesota and Wisconsin toward the river mill towns below St. Paul.

With the children preoccupied, Constance and Mr. Knight agreed upon a story they hoped would satisfy Constance's widowed Aunt Libby and other townspeople. Only those in their coach knew of the impromptu wedding ceremony. The reverend and the children readily agreed not to volunteer the fact that the wedding occurred on the train. The newly married couple would say they had met in Chicago—not an untruth as they met through Effie and Evan before the train left that great city.

"I hate deceit."

The vehemence of Mr. Knight's statement, coming between clenched teeth, shocked Constance. His jaw was rigid and his brown eyes glittered with suppressed rage.

It was a moment before she could rally to reply, "Surely it is necessary in this case. Anyone knowing the circumstances would understand the need for the untruths."

His gaze met hers, and his expression softened somewhat. "It distresses me that you and the children were drawn into the quarrel between Rasmus Pierce and myself. So like him to hide behind children. If it weren't for the twins' safety, I would never have agreed to the ceremony."

Of course he wouldn't, Constance reassured herself.

"I shall never be able to thank you sufficiently for disrupting your plans in order to save my nephew's and niece's lives. I have no doubt Mr. Pierce would enforce his threat against them."

"Unfortunately, Rasmus is capable of any act, no matter how reprehensible."

From the criminal's profile at the Pinkerton agency, Constance knew it was true. "Do you know him well?"

He snorted. "As well as anyone would wish to know a rattlesnake. We both grew up in River's Edge. He was always a shiftless bully. Even as a small boy he loved to see others cringe before him, would shove the weaker boys about and terrify the girls, destroying their toys and school books. Left school after the fifth grade level. Always wanted something for nothing. If he'd put half the effort into legitimate business he has into his criminal enterprises, he could be a successful, respected man by now."

"Yes, most criminals could, or so—so I've always believed." The theft and marriage ceremony must have shaken her more than she realized. She'd almost said that Mr. Pinkerton shared Mr. Knight's belief that many criminals had the power of mind to become honorable members of society if won from their evil ways.

"Miss Ward, I hope. . ."

Color rose to both their hairlines as they realized she was no longer Miss Ward. Their mutual embarrassment was relieved when Effie and Evan chorused, "The bridge! We're crossing the bridge!"

Indeed the clacking of the wheels against the steel changed subtly to a ringing clang as they moved out over the river. Relief cooled Constance's cheeks as the children's eager questions drew Justin across the narrow aisle.

The train whistle blasted through the car and moments later they arrived at the depot, a charming building with dormers in a steeply sloped roof trimmed with gingerbread. Through the window, Constance could see her graying, middle-aged Aunt Libby, reticule swinging from the hands clasped in front of her waist. Her frothy, lemon-colored gown and large hat looked frivolous on her slim-as-a-pin body with its wrinkled, almost gaunt face which ended in a jutting chin.

Constance couldn't help but smile. Trust Aunt Libby to be as up-to-date as tomorrow's newspaper. "A businesswoman in fashion must set an example if she wishes to win the women of the community," she'd said more than once while in Chicago on buying trips for her millinery.

Her grin died. What would Aunt Libby think when her niece arrived as Mrs. Justin Knight? She caught her breath at the name blazing through her thoughts.

"Aren't you coming?"

She turned at Effie's question. Mr. Knight was standing in the aisle and had opened the slotted mahogany doors above the windows to remove his duck valise and her black leather satchel with nickel plate trimmings.

Within minutes, they were descending to the platform. Aunt Libby threw out her gloved hands and rushed toward them, her high-heeled shoes clattering across the narrow wooden planks, the hem of her frothy gown moving like a cloud about her feet. She caught the children in her arms, her pale blue eyes glistening with unshed tears, her pointed chin quivering.

"You poor, poor dears! How wonderful to see you!" The crooning voice broke on the words. The children were momentarily lost in the folds of her voluminous gown.

Constance would have laughed at the sight if she weren't so concerned with explaining her new status. She felt her hand claimed by Mr. Knight and drawn securely through his arm.

Keeping her gaze on Libby, she swallowed hard and made herself ask the question burning in her mind. "Are. . .are you expecting the twins and me to stay in your home?"

His hand tightened over hers. "I've been fruitlessly casting about in my mind for an alternative, but in light of Rasmus' threat to the children, I don't believe we have any other options." His voice was low enough that she was certain no one else heard him. "Ma'am." The urgency in his tone drew her gaze to his. "I assure you, my actions shall in no wise compromise your honor."

Was it pity lying in the depths of his eyes? She wasn't accustomed to being pitied, and found that she didn't like it.

Aunt Libby released the children, and hurried toward

Constance. She was glad of the excuse to free her hand from Mr. Knight's arm to yield to Libby's embrace.

"It is so good to see you once more," she said earnestly.

"And you." Steel gray brows arched in obvious curiosity as Libby nodded to Justin. "Good evening. Returning from a business trip, I presume?"

His smile could charm a fox from its hole, Constance thought watching him remove his derby and greet Libby.

"Not completely business, Mrs. Ward. The trip afforded a great deal of pleasantry." One of his hands touched Constance's back lightly. "Your niece and I met in Chicago. I hope you will be pleased to hear that she is now my wife."

Libby struggled valiantly to remain a lady under the surprising news. "Why, I thought you. . ." Libby's shocked blue gaze met Constance's green eyes. Then her chin rose. Her smile deepened the multitude of wrinkles in her cheeks, but Constance saw the questions remaining in her eyes. "I couldn't be more pleased that marriage to Constance has brought you into the family, Mr. Knight."

He leaned down to kiss Libby's bright red cheek. "I was hoping you'd feel that way, Mrs. Ward. May I call you Aunt Libby?"

Constance caught her bottom lip between her teeth to keep from laughing at her aunt's flustered response. "Why. . .why, if you wish, Mr. Knight."

"Thank you. And I am Justin. If you'll excuse me, I must arrange for the horse-drawn bus to take us home."

"You are welcome to use the carriage I've rented. Of course, you will wish Effie and Evan to stay with me. You are on your honeymoon, after all."

"Oh, no!" Did her exclamation sound as desperate to her aunt as it did to her, Constance wondered. "We prefer the children to stay with us, Aunt Libby. I apologize for the inconvenience you've been put to arranging for our visit, but. . ."

She looked pleadingly at Mr. Knight.

He took Libby's gloved hand solicitously and nodded toward the express car, where the local sheriff had joined the crowd of railroad personnel and curious bystanders. "Perhaps you've noticed the excitement. I wouldn't wish to upset you, but there was a robbery a few miles from town." Libby's flat, lace-covered chest rose with her sharp gasp. "The children were quite disturbed by the event. Under the circumstances, we feel it would be best to keep them with us. I'm sure you understand."

"Naturally." A tremor shook the one word reply. Libby pulled a lace-trimmed handkerchief from her reticule and mopped her skinny face. "My, it is certainly a day of surprises, isn't it?"

Constance rested a hand on Libby's forearm. "Will you be all right, dear?"

Libby waved her hand away with bony fingers. "Think I haven't had a few surprises in my lifetime? None have conquered me yet."

Mr. Knight's laugh boomed out. Constance decided she quite liked the sound of it.

When he had retreated toward the pile of trunks, boxes and valises a short way down the platform, Constance said, "Would you watch the children for me? I must send a telegram to friends in Chicago. I promised to let them know when I arrived."

Hurrying toward the station house, Constance mentally pieced together the telegram she would send. It was true it was to be sent to friends, the female Pinkerton operatives with whom she shared a home in Chicago when not living elsewhere on a case. She wouldn't dare to send it directly to the office, for fear of revealing her true identity and purpose to the wire operator. It took some doing to come up with a message that told of the robbery, the marriage, and how she could be reached without revealing her position as an operative, but she was accustomed to such challenges.

The others were ready to leave when she returned to the carriage. Libby caught her in her arms when they dropped the woman at her own home.

"I'm so happy for you, dear. See that you stop by the shop tomorrow and tell me everything." She kissed the children good-bye, and stood beside the street waving until the buggy turned a corner and was lost to sight.

Effie and Evan eagerly pointed at town sights from the back seat as they drove along. The smell of the river and the smoke from the lumber mills filled the air. Children played in the neat yards they passed, young matrons pushed parasol-topped perambulators along the sidewalks, and carriages and delivery wagons met them on the street, the townspeople often waving and calling out greetings to Justin.

"It appears to be a pleasant town," Constance murmured. Perhaps making conversation would chase away the fear clawing at her stomach. Nothing in her previous experience had prepared her to move into a stranger's home as his wife.

"I've found it so. But I expect I'm prejudiced, having lived here all my twenty-six years. The town is about forty years old. The river has made it a profitable place. It's primarily logs that keep the town finances going. You saw the barges piled with them when we crossed the river. The way the northern woods have been logged off over the years with no replanting, it won't be long before the industries relying on them will begin dying."

Was he trying to calm her by rattling on so?

Libby's two-story frame home had been pleasant looking, but built on a somewhat small lot in a common part of town. Now Constance saw that they were moving into a wealthier neighborhood. Large lots with spacious homes gently met the wide street. "Even the horses' hoofs seem quieter against the pavement here," she remarked.

"Wooden blocks have been laid beneath the pavement to lessen the noise of horses and carriages passing."

He stopped the carriage beside a horse stoop. "This is my home."

While he climbed down and secured the horse to the cast iron ring beside the stoop, Constance glanced in surprise at the new, clapboard and stone Queen Anne house. It sprawled across the huge lot, jutting and receding seemingly at random. No area of the building remained flat for more than a few feet. A three-story tower with bay windows in the first two stories stood at one front corner. An open arcade rimmed with white railings in arched openings beneath a cone-shaped roof topped the tower. A wide porch with a matching white railing ran like a wavy shoreline along the first floor, above a latticework-covered foundation. Some windows were rectangular, some arched, others round. A brick chimney stack rose from the midst of the building.

It was a grand example of the popular extreme architecture of the day, but Constance couldn't relate the house to the man she thought Mr. Knight to be. Without giving it conscious consideration, she'd assumed he would live in a home similar to the one next door, a more masculine, quietly elegant red brick Colonial Revival with stately white columns.

"Is this where we are to stay?" Effie asked when Mr. Knight lifted her from the carriage. "Is this whole house yours?"

"Effie!"

"Yes," Mr. Knight's amused voice cut into Constance's low protest. "The whole house."

The children's eyes met and they grinned. Constance stomach tightened in apprehension. She'd seen that conspiratorial grin before. She took Effie's hand firmly. "I expect you and Evan to behave like a little lady and gentleman."

"Yes, ma'am."

"Yes, ma'am."

Their joint agreement didn't reassure her for a moment. She kept Effie's hand in her own as they started up the walk. Experience had taught her that if Effie was subdued, Evan's proper behavior was assured.

Mr. Knight opened one of the double doors with etched glass windows, and invited his companions to enter. Constance tried to ignore the anxiety which tightened her stomach. When she was attracted to this man earlier, she never thought she'd be married to him by day's end!

The size and elegance of the foyer fairly took Constance's breath. Marble covered the floor, rich mahogany lined the walls, an elegant gas and electric chandelier hung from the second-story ceiling which was covered in a fresco of clouds and cherubs against a robin's-egg blue sky. A wide stairway curved invitingly upward between gleaming mahogany posts.

"Justin, welcome home!"

A dainty blonde woman dashed toward them, her pink organdy gown drifting across the marble. A wave of lily of the valley scent surrounded her. The delicate features above a pointed chin were radiant with welcome as she held out tiny hands to Mr. Knight. He took them immediately, but stared at her as though in a trance.

This is the girl he loves, Constance thought with a pang.

A sweet laugh rang through the hall.

"I see I succeeded in surprising you. I've planned a homecoming dinner. Mrs. Kelly has helped me. Please don't scold. I know this won't be my home until Sunday, but it was such fun planning the dinner."

"Of course I'll not scold, Marian. It was just unexpected, seeing you here." He was pale beneath his wavy hair, and Constance's heart went out to him. To have to face his fiancee so soon!

Marian tucked a tiny hand beneath his arm possessively and smiled at Constance. "He never can bring himself to reprimand me. A wonderful quality in a man, don't you agree?" Not waiting for a reply, she looked up at Justin. "Aren't you going to introduce me to your friends?"

"Why don't the children and I look about your yard while you and Miss Marian greet each other?" Constance suggested.

Relief and gratitude relaxed his face. "There's a stable and carriage house out back. Perhaps the children would like to see the horses."

"Oh, yes!"

"Can we, Aunt Constance?"

"Of course, dears," she replied, leading them through the door. "Good evening, Miss Marian."

"Good evening." The confusion in Marian's voice cut an unexpected mark of guilt into Constance's heart. Why should she care that the girl, she couldn't be more than nineteen, should be hurt? The marriage had been necessary to protect the children, if not to save Mr. Knight's life. In her work, subterfuge was often required in apprehending the criminal element. Never had it disturbed her before.

But as she followed the children around the rambling house to the stable, she felt uncomfortably as though her principles were decidedly smudged.

three

Justin Knight stood in the open door and watched Marian rush down the lane. The wide-brimmed hat which matched her pink gown tilted unfashionably, teetered as though about to fall. She hadn't taken time to secure it before rushing from the house.

She had, however, taken the time to throw a choice porcelain figurine in his direction, fortunately with poor aim, and tell him exactly what she thought of a man who would wed another woman two days before he was to marry her. His face still burned from her contempt. It didn't help any that he agreed with her every sentiment.

The familiar scent of her lily of the valley fragrance lingered in the air that still reverberated with her anger. He hated like fury to hurt and humiliate her. He wished things were different; wished Rasmus hadn't effectually barred him from telling her the truth about his marriage by threatening the children.

His fist struck the mahogany door with a force that set the leaded, etched glass trembling. How he hated deceit!

Yet if excitable Marian discovered the true reason for his marriage, she would never be able to keep her knowledge of it from Rasmus. The toe of his shoe brushed at the fragments of broken figurine covering the marble floor, a tangible reminder of the whirlwind Marian created when he told her he had married someone else.

His lips stretched in a tight grimace. May as well admit the guilt he was fighting wasn't only over Rasmus' enforced deceit. A man in his position should feel he'd lost the most precious of life's gifts. He didn't.

His affection for Marian had never been the overwhelming

attraction of which he'd heard so many men speak regarding the women they married. When he was the only remaining bachelor amongst his friends, he'd decided he'd overestimated the emotions involved with love.

At twenty-six, he sometimes felt like an old man. Since taking over the bank when his parents died in a train accident three years ago, he hadn't much time for youth's light-hearted pursuits. Being with Marian, who faced life eagerly, made him feel young again. And so he'd proposed to her.

Even so, he'd never told Marian he loved her and she'd never asked for his love. Had he been unfair to her, asking her to share his life without loving her more than life?

Regardless, it was behind him now. He was married to Constance.

Even if his parents hadn't drilled into him the belief that marriage vows were inviolate, his own commitment to the Lord left him with the same conclusion. He stuffed his fists into the pockets of his gray trousers. The circumstances of the ceremony didn't change the sanctity of the vows.

At least he'd had the opportunity to tell Marian of his marriage before she heard it from someone else.

"Thank Thee for that, Lord. Help her through this time."

The broken engagement would be difficult for her pride if not her emotions. It would be socially embarrassing for her and her family. Anger burned through him. *And Rasmus would bring such pain on Marian in the name of love!*

A mirthless laugh jolted from his lips. He'd always been so conservative. Marrying a woman he'd known less than a day and taking responsibility for her and two children, one could hardly call that staid.

"Beggin' yer pardon, Mr. Knight."

He turned to face the short, round, middle-aged woman with deep red hair piled above her face. Tantalizing odors of oyster stew and roasting beef clung about her.

The woman must have heard Marian's temper tantrum, he realized at the sight of her flaming cheeks. Her plump hands were settled above her stomach on the thin linen apron covering her cotton house dress. Disapproval oozed from every pore of her face.

"What is it, Mrs. Kelly?"

"The meal Miss Marian was havin' me prepare for ye—will ye be wantin' it?"

He smiled into the eyes stuffed beneath thick red brows. "Is there enough for two adults and two hungry children?"

She drew her short self up straighter. "Have ye ever known there ta be a lack of food on me table?"

"Not once in all the years you've cooked for me." It felt good to chuckle. "Before dinner, would you clean up this mess in which we're standing? Also, my wife and her niece and nephew are in the backyard. Please ask them to come inside. If Terrence, the stable boy, hasn't gone home for the night, ask him to bring the bags from the carriage before returning it to the livery."

She bustled down the marble hallway toward the kitchen, the large bow of her apron dancing on her ample hips.

Justin entered the parlor, his frowning glance taking in the new, luxurious furnishings chosen by Marian. So many items for which he had yet to pay. Marian had cut no corners with their prospective home, he thought. He'd given her a spending limit, but he'd been so busy with the bank that he hadn't thought to see that she kept within it. She'd spent extravagantly. He'd thought he had enough to cover the debts she'd accumulated when he started home from Chicago. Rasmus' robbery of the express car was going to complicate his ability to meet those bills.

The thought crossed his mind again an hour later when he led Constance and the children into the room following dinner. He pushed a wall button, brightening the large, high-ceiling room with electric light from the cut-glass chandelier.

He watched Constance's gaze run swiftly over the pale gold patterned wallpaper topped by the wide, hand-painted frieze of blue and gold, to the tasseled, dark blue fabric window cornices over the soft golden draperies in the bay window. Beneath them stood a long, graceful rosewood sofa covered in blue damask. Matching chairs sat opposite the fireplace, where an elegant brass and crystal clock was chiming the hour of nine upon the silk lambrequin covering the mantle. A mass of fresh flowers filled the room with fragrance from a crystal vase upon a marble-topped, elegantly carved rosewood table beneath the chandelier. The Persian rug brought bright splashes of red into the otherwise softly-colored room.

"I like your house, Mr. Knight," Effie said decidedly. "May Evan and I explore the rest of it?"

"Effie!"

She lifted her eyebrows innocently at Constance. "But I said 'may we'."

Justin scuttled a laugh. He was sure Constance wouldn't appreciate his undermining of her disciplinary attempts. "Tomorrow you may explore to your heart's content, but just now I'd like to speak with you."

When Constance and the children were seated on the sofa, he pulled a matching gentleman's chair close. Leaning forward, elbows on his thighs, fingers linked loosely between his knees, he smiled at Effie and Evan.

"Have you ever been to Sunday School?"

They nodded in unison.

"We learn lots of Bible verses there," Effie offered. "I can say more verses than anyone else in our class. Evan can say almost as many, though."

"Do you remember learning that we must forgive our enemies, and those who hurt us?"

Effie nodded vigorously, but Justin noticed that Evan's nod

wasn't nearly as eager, and his large brown eyes were wary.

"You were both very brave on the train today when Mr. Pierce stopped to talk with us."

Evan jerked up straight, his back no longer touching the sofa. "He was a mean man! He pointed a gun at me!"

Constance laid an arm over his wide sailor collar. Her eyes met Justin's, and he cringed inside at the pain he saw there for the children.

"And you did exactly the right thing when Mr. Pierce did that, Evan," he continued. "Perhaps you remember in your Bible stories that when Jesus was taken prisoner and his enemies accused him, Jesus answered them not a word. Sometimes keeping silent, as you did today, is wise. There's more wise things we can do, even though Mr. Pierce isn't present."

Evan leaned slowly back against the sofa once more. "What?" he asked tentatively.

Effie, sitting on the edge of the cushion swinging her feet, held her hands palms upward. "Yes, what?"

"We can pray for him." His was watching Evan, but he noticed the jerk of Constance's head toward him at his comment. A sadness slipped through him. On top of everything else that had happened, was he married to a woman who didn't revere the Lord? Perhaps he misunderstood her action. Perhaps she did follow God and was surprised to find that he did, too. *Well, there'll be time to explore that later.*

"Rasmus Pierce is older than you children. He's bigger and he has a gun. But you are stronger and richer than Mr. Pierce."

"We are?" Effie grinned.

Evan just continued looking at him skeptically.

"You are. Because you love Jesus. When you have Jesus beside you, it doesn't matter how tough things seem, because Jesus is stronger than anything or anyone. And He's promised to never leave those who love Him."

Effie nodded. "We learned that in Sunday School."

Evan nodded slowly. Justin breathed a small sigh of relief. Was he beginning to reach the boy? Evan had been as tense as a wound up tin top ever since Rasmus drew his gun. Not that he could blame him. But he couldn't bear to think of the boy living in a world of fear because of Rasmus.

"We can pray for Rasmus. We can ask God to forgive him, and make him His child."

"Yes, let's!" Effie's curls bounced in the light.

Evan nodded slowly, pushing himself forward on the cushion. "I'll pray."

"All right, old man." Justin bowed his head, then peeked to see what the children were doing. Both had their heads lowered solemnly over folded hands, their eyes squeezed shut. Constance's troubled gaze was on Evan.

"Dear God," Evan began, and Justin shut his eyes. "Please forgive Mr. Pierce for bein' a bad man and pointin' his gun at us and robbin' the train. Make him love Jesus so he'll be a good man. Amen."

"A-men," Effie repeated.

Evan's anxious brown eyes were waiting for his own when Justin lifted his head. "Will he be a good man now, and not point guns at boys?"

Justin pressed his lips together firmly. He wasn't going to find it so easy himself to forgive Rasmus for frightening the children. But even if he had the luxury of refusing to forgive the thief, he couldn't afford to set an example of unforgiveness for Evan. If the boy held hatred and fear to himself it would only make the harm Rasmus had done worse and longlasting.

He swallowed hard. "Sometimes it takes a long time for God to finish His work in a man. It might be quite a while before Mr. Pierce learns to love Jesus. But we'll keep praying for him, won't we?"

"Yes," Evan said in a low voice. "But I wish God would work quick."

Justin grinned as he stood. "One thing we can count on, old man; God's time is always best, even when it seems slow to us. By the time on that brass clock on the mantle, it's getting mighty late for small boys and girls to be up. You'd best be getting to bed."

Constance slipped a hand on each of the children's shoulders. He liked the brave, sweet smile she gave them.

"I'll go up with you. Say goodnight to Mr. Knight."

"Miss Ward, when you're done, please meet me in the library."

He thought for a moment she would refuse, but finally she inclined her head.

It was a half hour before she came to the library that served as his study. He rose behind his desk and watched as she examined the room from the doorway.

This woman is my wife. The thought set his heart quick-stepping. She was lovely! Not in Marian's bright, bubbly manner, but in a gentle yet self-confident manner that surrounded her in an aura of serenity. The light from the gasolier glowed off her thick black hair swept to the back of her head in a delightfully simple but elegant twist.

From the beginning he'd been fascinated by her eyes. Unexpectedly, deeply green, clearer than emeralds. More unexpectedly, they met one's gaze frankly, without the proper dropping of lashes or the twinkling of a flirtatious tease. They were eyes to be trusted. "The heart of her husband doth safely trust in her." The verse from Proverbs 31 slipped across his mind. It fit this woman.

Since meeting her in Chicago (could it truly have been only this morning?) he'd wanted to know more of her, rejoicing in the bits and pieces that were revealed in his conversations with her and the children during the twelve hours on the train.

Each time they'd shared a smile over the children's antics, a warm joy rippled through him. It was as though his heart had tumbled to her and was no longer in his keeping. The knowledge had left a burning ache in his chest. Why did she come into his life now, when he had no right to be attracted to her? He had asked the Lord to forgive him, had tried to keep his eyes from her face, his ears from listening for her voice.

And now she was his wife.

What did she think of all that had happened today, drawing her to his home as his bride? When they'd stopped before the house, he'd thought he recognized fright staring starkly at him momentarily from her wide eyes, and fury with Rasmus had raged within him.

"What a comforting room. It appears much more like you than the rest of the house." Her warm, rich voice preceded her as she crossed the Brussels carpet of wine, gold, and brown toward his desk.

His neck and face burned. Had he been staring blatantly at her all this time? "Marian designed and furbished the house, except for this room and my bedchamber. I insisted on having my way with those."

She stopped near the inlaid desk, her fingers linked lightly together in front of her straight black skirt of moire silk. "That explains it, then. Your house is fine and beautiful, but I thought it unlike you. It is like Marian; bright and gay and especially choice."

"You are most kind."

"But I believe I prefer this room. The bookcases filled with volumes behind the leaded glass doors, the wine velvet draperies, the leather furniture, the frieze that matches the border of the carpet. They fill the room with welcome and warmth."

She stepped closer to the bookshelves beside them to examine the volumes. He liked her peaceful ways, her low, gentle, rich voice, the graceful way she moved without ever appearing to rush, her quiet hands. Marian's hands were in constant motion; she never seemed to rest.

"You have a wide array of interests, judging by your books. Longfellow, Thoreau, James Fenimore Cooper, Mark Twain, Dickens, History of France, a journal by Lt. Zebulon Pike, and several volumes by Allan Pinkerton." She glanced over her shoulder. Was there veiled amusement in her eyes? "Didn't Mr. Pinkerton found the Pinkerton National Detective Agency?"

"Yes. His works aren't particularly literary, but he does describe common methods used by bank robbers, forgers, counterfeiters and such, which I've found useful in my position with the bank."

He cleared his throat and stepped out from behind the desk, indicating the long leather sofa beneath the doublewide window on the opposite wall. "Won't you be seated, Miss—may I call you Constance? I'm afraid people will consider it odd if I continue addressing you as Miss Ward, and I'm sure you would prefer to be called Mrs. Knight only when necessary."

Color flooded her face above the high black lace collar, but she answered steadily.

"Thank you. Under the circumstances, Constance will be acceptable."

She lowered herself gracefully onto the sofa, her straight back not touching the upholstery. He settled himself at the other end of the sofa, allowing a comfortable, nonthreatening distance between them.

"On the train, you and the children told me a little about yourselves and your trip. I know you are all from Chicago, the children's mother died years ago and their father almost six months ago; that you were traveling to River's Edge to visit your aunt, Mrs. Libby Ward. Beyond that, I know very little."

Her green eyes met his with complete composure. "There is little else to tell. Aunt Libby and I are the last of our family. I could hardly raise the children alone. Who would stay with them when they were not at school and I was at work? Aunt Libby offered to give the children a home. Between her and

Mrs. Chandler, Aunt Libby's housemate, the children could be cared for more properly."

"There is no young man you pledged to marry who would share the responsibility of the children with you?" At her slight drawing back, he hastened on, "I assure you, I wouldn't ask such a personal question on our short acquaintance under other circumstances. This situation is untenable for you, to say the least, and I only hope that it will not also damage a friendship which is important to you."

"I am promised to no young man."

Had she hesitated before answering? Was there perhaps a man who had not asked for her hand, but who carried her heart? He hoped fervently not, for her sake as well as his own. Wasn't she enduring enough already because of him?

She leaned toward him slightly, her hands clutched in her lap. "I am most distressed that your marriage to Miss Marian has been interrupted. I do hope she will forgive you when Rasmus Pierce is behind bars and the truth is revealed. Naturally, we shall then obtain an annulment, and. . ."

"There will be no annulment."

Her eyes met his, shock glinting off their green depths. "Pardon me?"

He'd been hoping to avoid this discussion for a few days. Well, may as well get it behind them.

"There will be no annulment."

four

Constance shot to her feet. It took all her training to keep her voice low and even rather than shouting at the top of her lungs as she wished.

"No annulment? Surely you jest."

He stood also, meeting her gaze evenly. She wished he'd remained seated. It did nothing for her self-confidence to have him towering above her with his masculine strength well defined beneath his gray jacket.

"I assure you, I do not jest about vows taken before God. I am sorry your life has been inconvenienced, but. . ."

"Inconvenienced? You call it an inconvenience to be married to a man whom I have known less than twenty-four hours?"

"Have you so soon forgotten the vows we exchanged? 'Until death us do part.'"

Was she as pale as he? Even his lips were white. *He had been engaged to Marian,* she reminded herself; *he can't want this marriage to be real.* Her shoulders relaxed slightly beneath the black silk.

"Do you believe I shall betray the temporary nature of the marriage and endanger your life? Please rest assured I shall not. My niece and nephew's lives also stand in danger, you may recall."

"You've been stronger through this ordeal than I would have believed possible of any woman. I am certain you will not forget for a moment the danger that remains to the children. As I said, it is the vows. . ."

"Might I remind you that we were wed at gunpoint? As you yourself told Rasmus, no minister or judge would uphold such a marriage against the participants' wishes. Nor would the strictest of society's matrons expect such a marriage to be honored."

"*I* expect to honor my vows."

His quiet tone frightened her; it was chillingly convincing.

"Regardless of my feelings in the matter? Regardless of the disruption to my life and the children's? I cannot believe a highly principled man would insist on binding an unwilling stranger to himself. Do you feel it is your faith which requires this?"

"Yes." He seemed surprised she would even ask.

"Isn't God supposed to be just? Yet you have asked forgiveness for a criminal, and believe God would force strangers to honor vows exchanged at gunpoint! I do not understand your God."

"*My* God? Aren't you a believer?"

"I . . . I . . .are you now challenging my faith?" She wasn't a believer. In these enlightened times, it was embracing ignorance to accept the beliefs of past centuries in a God who created and ruled the world, she thought. Yet she knew she would win no favor or respect from this man by expressing her views.

"Do you believe I am a heathen because I do not feel compelled to remain married to you for the rest of my life? I assure you, under normal circumstances, I, too, believe in the sanctity of marriage."

"If you had believed our marriage to be permanent, would you have entered into it?"

She stared at him, wanting desperately to say she would not have married him under such circumstances. Even as instantly attracted to him as she'd been, in her wildest imaginings she wouldn't have considered marrying a stranger.

Yet. . .she took a deep breath, dropped her gaze to the colorful Brussels carpet, then raised it again to his, squaring her shoulders.

"If it were the only way to save the children's lives, or yours, yes, I would have entered into the marriage even believing it to be permanent."

His eyes widened slightly at her admission that she would have entered into the marriage even to save him. Had he thought she would allow a man to be killed if it was within her power to prevent it?

The stoniness in his chestnut brown eyes softened. "It is all right then."

Whatever could he mean, she wondered, but he continued before she could ask.

"There is nothing to be gained from continuing this discussion. Are we agreed that until Rasmus Pierce is under lock and key, and solidly under, the marriage must at least appear permanent?"

"Yes," she agreed grudgingly. "Is it possible the minister is an accomplice of Rasmus Pierce?" Recalling the timid, trembling man, she doubted it, but she would grasp at any straw at this point.

"You mean, could he be an impostor? I'm afraid not." There was gentleness in his voice and pity in his eyes. "I know his face. He's been serving at a church in Red Wing, a few miles north of here, for five years or more."

"I see."

"It has been a long day. You must be exhausted."

The thought she had suppressed since the vows were exchanged pushed its way to the forefront of her mind. Her breath seemed to stop, though her heart hammered on faster and louder than ever beneath her tailored black silk bodice. He'd explained during dinner that he only employed day servants, so not even Mrs. Kelly would be in the home this evening. She had thought Mr. Knight too fine to insist that. . . She couldn't complete the thought. Had she been mistaken? If he considered the marriage permanent, would he expect. . . ?

"Your bags have been taken to your room, which is beside the children's. My room adjoins yours." He pulled his hand from his pocket and held out a key. "This is the only key to the door connecting our rooms."

Her lungs almost hurt from her breath of relief as she accepted the key.

"Thank you," she murmured. Almost immediately she knew her relief was for more than her own physical safety. She would have hated to find Justin Knight was not the honorable man she had instinctively believed.

The realization frightened her. She was trained not to trust people; trained to believe anyone capable of deceit. How, why, had she allowed this man to penetrate her usual defenses?

She explored the discomforting thought further in her room as she worked over her required daily report to the Pinkerton agency. It shook her to the core to realize that she'd let her guard down with Justin. To do so was extremely dangerous. If an operative trusted the wrong person, it could mean death to oneself and others. Never had she allowed herself the luxury of trust in the past, not beyond her family and fellow agents.

She replaced the silver pen in its ornate holder on the graceful mahogany writing desk which stood beneath the double windows draped in pale blue damask. The material matched that on the chaise lounge at the end of the lace-canopied bed and the bench before the vanity whose top was covered with delicate silver appointments. One of these was a fragile atomizer filled with lily of the valley fragrance such as Marian was wearing earlier. She herself hadn't worn scent since becoming an agent. It was too distinctive for someone who must change identities frequently and remain in the background more often than not.

It is a lovely room for a bride, Constance admitted, observing it as she rose. *What joyful anticipation Marian must have known in decorating it! How awful for her to have her plans in tatters!*

She fingered the delicate cream lace draping a bedpost. For that matter, wasn't her own life in tatters? She, who had always prided herself on the control she had over her life. Who had pitied friends whose lives were dictated by their fathers or husbands. Not for her a life such as that.

How she'd enjoyed being a Pinkerton operative! The excitement of knowing she was helping the cause of justice. She hadn't been tempted once to exchange it for marriage, even though she'd now reached the rather advanced age of twenty-three. The agency had a strict policy against the employment of married women.

She *might* have been tempted to marry Alex otherwise. He was such fun when they worked on cases together. He had a brilliant mind for counteracting criminals, and was a wonder at acting the parts necessary in their cases.

Although they had never courted because it was against agency policy for agents to see each other romantically, he *had* asked her to marry him when her brother Charles died. She had refused.

Occasionally, she'd allowed herself to wonder what it would be like to spend her life with Alex. There was no one she knew with whom she would prefer to be married. But she certainly wasn't ready to give up control of her life to any man yet.

She pushed away from the bedpost impatiently. "Well, it certainly appears you have done so!" she whispered, crossing to the window to peer unseeingly out at the large back lawn flanked by the stable and carriage house.

Lately her life had careened more and more out of her control, culminating in this afternoon's fiasco. Within the last six months, her brother Charles died, she'd been left with the care of his children, and now she was married to a stranger, and her career was threatened.

"All things work together for good to them that love God."

Constance gave an unfeminine snort as the quote slipped uninvited into her mind. The thought might be comforting, if she loved God.

Charles had loved God. He'd taught Effie and Evan to love Him, also. Charles had tried to convince her that she was a sinner in need of God's love and the salvation He offered through His Son, Jesus Christ.

She'd only laughed at him. A sinner? She set high ideals for herself. Her life was devoted to bringing lawbreakers to justice. Surely if there was a just God, He would have to admit she had done everything humanly possible to become a good person. What more could He expect of her?

Honesty.

The word shot through her mind, burned into her heart. Her very spirit seemed to writhe in discomfort. Loyalty to the law was her highest ideal. Honesty, unfortunately, was often forsaken in her commitment to justice.

Justin had hated to be dishonest, even to save his own life and that of the children. She could still hear the distaste in his voice as he'd spoken of his hatred for deceit.

She was unaccustomed to people who held themselves to such a high standard of integrity. As a detective, she dealt regularly with criminals to whom truth was foreign. In order to trap them, it was common for her and other operatives to pretend to be people they weren't and to make promises they had no intention of keeping.

This marriage was only another of many roles. It was unreasonable for her and Justin to consider their vows unbreakable under the circumstances. Yet she couldn't help but admire his insistence on keeping them. To do so would mean losing the woman he loved, and taking responsibility for herself and the children 'til death us do part.' In the face of such self-sacrifice, she felt almost unworthy beside him.

She tried to shed the thought with her wrapper, but it remained to climb with her between the crisp new sheets slightly scented with lily of the valley. The deep lace trimming the top sheet tickled her chin as she drew it up. She wished she felt as clean inside as the bed linens felt to her. Always she'd been proud of her high ideals. It was extremely uncomfortable feeling unworthy. She didn't care for it, not one whit.

❧

Justin watched Constance leave the library. His brows puckered. Had he been unspeakably cruel, insisting there be no annulment? *The day must have been murderous for her, valiant though she'd been through the improbable events.*

A wry smile twisted his lips. This was his wedding night, and he and his bride had spent the evening discussing an annulment. His admiration for the woman who was now his wife had multiplied as they talked. Even though horror, then anger, had followed disbelief in her eyes at his sudden declaration, her voice hadn't risen from its rich, low tones.

He tugged a chain and plunged the room into darkness before crossing to a window to stare out at the black night. Did he have any right to expect Constance to act according to his beliefs, to spend the rest of her life with him, simply because she had been on a certain train at a certain moment in time? But always he'd believed a marriage vow unbreakable. If she chose to leave him when Rasmus was apprehended. . . . His heart contracted painfully at the thought. If she chose to leave, he'd remain true to his vow.

The thought of a future without a loving companion beside him left him feeling as alone as a man on an ice floe.

"All things work together for good to them that love God." He clutched at the hope in the promise.

five

"How many boats do you count, Evan? I count twelve!"

Constance and Justin exchanged smiles at Effie's exuberance. The child stood on tiptoe in the open third floor of the corner tower, her hands clutching the six-inch-wide railing topping the short wall. Even with their lithe little bodies stretched to their limits, the twins were barely tall enough to see out the arch which was open to the weather.

A good thing, Constance thought. If the wall were shorter, Effie's enthusiasm might endanger her. The way she threw herself at life, one day that child would land in a powerful lot of trouble, or Constance missed her guess.

"I count thirteen boats," Evan answered after his usual careful deliberation of the situation. He pointed a thin little finger toward where the river rounded a bend to be hidden from their view. "See that towboat comin'?"

"It wasn't there when I counted," Effie informed him with a toss of her curls.

The sound of Justin strangling a laugh brought Constance's gaze to his face, half hidden behind one of his large hands. The laugh sparkling in his eyes slipped into sadness as he looked out toward the ribbon of water.

"One day there won't be many boats left on the Mississippi. The railroads are taking over the transporting of goods and passengers which are the lifeblood of river economy, even the transporting of the logs on which River's Edge's economy relies. Already the river traffic has diminished substantially."

She could think of nothing encouraging to say about his comments, so changed the subject.

"What do you call this area? It reminds one of a widow's walk, where a sea captain's wife would watch for her husband's return."

He shook his head slightly. "There is no special name for it."

"Look! A bird is sitting right beside me!" Effie's stage whisper should have scared the sparrow away, but it didn't. The tiny brown bird sat on the pot of bright geraniums inches from Effie's hand, turning its head this way and that as it viewed the giggling girl.

A river-scented breeze caught one of Effie's long brown curls, and the sparrow darted away. She spun around. "I'm going to call this room the Bird Cage!"

Justin nodded decidedly. "The Bird Cage it is."

Constance tucked behind her ear a stray lock of hair with which the breeze insisted upon playing. "The view is spectacular, most of the town, the wide expanse of water dotted with islands, and the beautiful craggy bluffs."

"There's an eyeglass in my office. I'll leave it here for your use," Justin offered. "Lieutenant Zebulon Pike explored this region in 1805, two years after the area was acquired by the United States. In describing the area he said, 'It was altogether a prospect so variegated and romantic that a man may scarcely expect to enjoy such a one but twice or thrice in the course of his life.'"

Hands on the gleaming white railing, her gaze drifted over the landscape. "I agree with the Lieutenant. It would be lovely to spend one's life in the midst of such beauty."

She turned to question him concerning an unusual building, but the words died in her throat at the unexpected, fervent light burning in the eyes watching her. *Whatever was he thinking?*

His attention was diverted by Evan tugging at his sleeve. "May Effie and me sleep out here, sir?"

"Effie and I," Constance corrected, as she did twenty times a day.

He nodded solemnly. "Yes, Effie and I. May we sleep out here?"

"Oh, yes! May we, Mr. Knight?" Effie was jumping up and down, unable to contain her enthusiasm.

"It might be cold," Constance suggested. "It will be dark, and there may be mosquitoes."

Effie waved her little hands in a dismissing motion. "We don't mind. Little things like that don't bother us."

"No, we wouldn't mind," Evan seconded in his serious tone.

Effie threw her arms about one of Justin's legs, almost throwing him off balance in her ardor. "*Please*, Mr. Knight! It would be *won*derful!"

"Your aunt and I will discuss it. Run along to your rooms and collect your hats. We're going to the business district."

Effie's whoops disappeared as the children ran through the house, the door to the Bird Cage slamming behind them.

"Those two might have your nice new home torn to bits within a few days."

His grin was pleasant. "Effie is quite a charmer. It isn't easy to resist her beseeching brown eyes."

Constance started to smile in sympathy, but the remembrance of Miss Marian's similar comment last evening stopped the smile cold. "He never can bring himself to reprimand me. A wonderful quality in a man." At the memory, a chill settled about her heart like a fog. It took her quite by surprise. *Why should I feel. . .almost jealous? How absurd!*

"There's something we forgot yesterday."

Instantly her nerve endings served warning. His voice was so smooth that she knew instantly he was about to broach a topic to which he feared she would object.

"The wonder would be if we did not forget something in the unprecedented melee."

He dug in a small vest pocket with his thumb and forefinger. A ring flashed in the fingers he held toward her, destroying the atmosphere of pleasant camaraderie.

Her hands clutched the railing the children had recently vacated, and she fought the wave of weakness that threatened. She'd faced guns in the hands of criminals with less fear.

"Surely that isn't necessary."

"You needn't stare at it in horror, as though it were a viper. It's only a wedding band."

"It. . .it makes everything seem so. . .permanent."

"Isn't that the image we wish to portray?"

They stared at each other, neither making a move to relent. After what seemed aeons, Justin asked gently, "Don't you believe, too, that it would be wiser to wear the ring? Truly?"

She gave in then, but couldn't gain command of her voice, so only nodded.

He took the hand she reluctantly extended and slipped the ring on her finger. It felt as heavy as the huge anchors she'd seen on steamboats.

He released her hand immediately and she let it fall back upon the railing. Sunshine danced off the gold band, drawing her gaze to it like a magnet. Delicate orange blossoms were etched about it, and the sight of them caught her heart in a little twinge. It was too sweet. She would have preferred a plain band. *Was this dear little ring the one he'd chosen for Miss Marian?* The thought repulsed her, but she daren't ask. He needed no reminders that he wasn't married to the woman of his choice.

"I took the liberty this morning of stopping by the newspaper office. Rasmus will be looking for an announcement. I spoke with my lawyer, also. We're to stop by his office this afternoon to sign the special marriage license. The judge is a friend of mine, so there was no difficulty obtaining it."

Did he think she would rejoice at the news? He had simply taken care of necessary details.

Simply. Among his friends, people who respected him. People who wouldn't understand his apparent ungentlemanly behavior toward Miss Marian. The least she could do was be civil.

"Thank you for looking to these details. It cannot be easy for you."

He leaned a hip against the short wall, ignoring her sympathy. "Marian had calling cards printed. You'll find them in the writing desk in your room."

She nodded. *Something else of Marian's. Of course she must use them. A lady needs calling cards, and it would be silly to go to the expense of printing others which would only say the same thing, Mrs. Justin Knight, or Mr. and Mrs. Justin Knight.* For a moment Constance felt as though she'd lost her identity, as though she'd been swallowed whole in Justin Knight's personality. Mrs. Justin Knight. The title left no inkling of the woman who was Constance Ward.

"Aunt Constance! Mr. Knight! Yoo-hoo!" Effie's yell from the yard below broke the uncomfortable silence.

"Coming!" Justin hollered between cupped hands.

Constance shook her head. "I despair of ever molding her into a lady."

"I confess I like her quite as she is."

So did Constance. It pleased her that he was fond of Effie, but she knew better than to believe her exuberant niece's manner would be acceptable as she matured.

The afternoon was more trying than Constance expected. Everywhere they went people stared. A number of matrons refused to respond to Justin's greetings, pursing their lips primly and shooting him disapproving looks from beneath their bonnets. Dusky color darkened his face at their actions. Constance's heart went out to him, and she lifted her chin slightly higher and made her smiles for him especially warm as they walked along the bustling streets.

He pointed out buildings of interest, shared pieces of the

town's past, his hopes for its future. He kept the conversation friendly without a hint of intimacy, and Constance discovered herself relaxing and enjoying an easy camaraderie.

The smell of the river and nearby lumber mills, and sounds of boat horns and whistles, added unusual elements to the air of the business section. The normal sounds and smells of the horses, carriages, delivery wagons, trolley cars and smokestacks couldn't hide the effect of living along the Mississippi.

When they passed the post office, Constance took the opportunity to post her report to headquarters, explaining to Justin casually that she'd written a short note to a friend the night before.

They stopped at his bank and he introduced Constance and the children to the officers and clerks. She glanced about with keen observation, noting with approval the discreetly cautious yet respectful manner with which his employees treated the bank's patrons. But she found it disconcerting to be introduced as his wife to the people with whom he worked intimately. Each hour, each introduction, added another snarl in the web of deceit begun with their marriage.

"Your aunt's millinery is only a few shops up the block," Justin said as they left the bank. He nodded toward a building on the opposite side of the street. "That general store is owned by Rasmus Pierce's parents."

Had he heard the catch of her breath at his revelation? She knew, of course, that Mr. Pierce's parents had a shop in River's Edge. It was for that reason her superintendent had been eager for her to bring the children to the town. She had been expected to work undercover, simply keeping her eyes and ears open, listening to local gossip, and managing an introduction to Mr. and Mrs. Pierce in the innocent position of Libby's niece. The children would not have been placed in danger if things had gone as planned.

Inside Libby's millinery, Justin shifted uncomfortably in the midst of the bonnets and trimmings. Constance viewed his discomfort with ill-concealed amusement. He soon announced he'd wait at the bank while she visited.

Upon Justin's departure, Libby requested her assistant, who had been busy trimming hats at a table piled high with hat forms, laces, ribbons, ostrich feathers, and silk flowers, to help Effie select a new bonnet, and Evan a new sailor hat. As soon as they were out of earshot, she demanded her niece tell all concerning the unexpected marriage.

Constance only smiled mysteriously, fingering the black silk roses bedecking the wide brim of a bonnet on a cast iron display stand.

"Surely you know the ways of love are unfathomable, Aunt Libby."

"Hmpf! If Mr. Knight hadn't been Marian's intended, I'd have thought it perfectly lovely to find you married to him. As it is, customers' heads and tongues have been wagging all morning."

"I'm sorry for any embarrassment caused you." The waves sent out by that abominable ceremony lapped everywhere.

Once the apology was received, Libby put the offense behind her.

"Never you mind, dear. I know you wouldn't intentionally act improperly. What is done is done. You are now Mrs. Justin Knight, and that is that." She bounced her palms off her skirt and looked Constance up and down. "My dear, hasn't your mourning for Charles ended yet? Surely the six months is nearly up."

Constance looked down at her black gown. "I've grown so accustomed to wearing mourning that I seldom notice it now. The six months were past last week, but I didn't even remember to bring anything but mourning wear from Chicago." If only mourning in one's heart could be put off so easily and at a socially prescribed time!

"Never you mind, dear. Mrs. Clayton, who rooms with me, has her garment shop next door. It will be great fun helping you select a new wardrobe."

"Oh, but I can't possibly afford an entire wardrobe! A few pieces, perhaps. Black silk is still considered proper and fashionable, is it not? The mourning gowns will be sufficient for most days."

"With the mourning period over and you the new bride of one of the town's wealthiest and most respected men? They certainly will not be sufficient. Mr. Knight can afford the finest wardrobe to be had for his wife, make no mistake."

"I shall certainly not allow Mr. Knight to purchase my wardrobe!" Constance swallowed her pride at the sight of Libby's shocked face. It wouldn't do to show an unnatural reluctance to spend her husband's funds. "A bride should supply her own trousseau," she finished lamely.

"At the threat of insulting you, my dear, I am quite certain you cannot afford the manner of wardrobe required by the wife of a man of Mr. Knight's stature."

Another unexpected complication! She had some funds, but she couldn't afford to spend all her money on clothing.

"You'll soon see I'm right about this. Until then, let me furnish you with some outfits." Libby held up a hand as Constance started to protest. "I hadn't the pleasure of purchasing an engagement or wedding gift. The least I can do is furnish a few pieces for your trousseau."

To that Constance agreed.

It was rather fun trying on new readymade garments, and selecting patterns for others from Mrs. Clayton's supply. She needed everything new, from undergarments out.

Libby held up a sheer yellow organdy with a wide, fluttery collar that settled lightly over huge sleeves. A yellow satin sash secured the waist. "This is just what you need, my dear. Women are either a flat or a fluff this season, according to the *New York World*." Her gaze ran over Constance's black gown contemptuously. "With your severely tailored outfits, you have been a flat at its most extreme. It's time you showed that new husband of yours that you are a woman."

The statement sent tingles along Constance's nerves. The last thing she needed was to remind her temporary husband of her femininity. Her fingers played with the delicate fabric of the collar. "It is lovely. But I'm afraid it's entirely inappropriate."

"Nonsense. This pale yellow, butter yellow it's called, is all the rage, and will set off your black hair to advantage."

"But. . ."

"I have not been in the business of fashion all these years without knowing what enhances a woman's best features. Now stop arguing and try this gown on. I declare, you are more difficult than little Effie."

Constance laughed softly to herself as she slipped into the frock. What would her fellow female operatives think if they saw how easily her aunt destroyed her resolve?

The gown is becoming, she admitted to herself, turning in front of the tall mirror. Libby was right. The color was perfect with her hair. She fingered the cream-colored lace edging the collar. She'd forgotten what color could do for a woman. What would Mr. Knight think of her in this gown? Dismay swept through her. What did it matter what Mr. Knight thought?

"Please help me out of this, Aunt Libby."

"I have a large, soft leghorn bonnet with all manner of flowers in my shop that will be perfect with the dress. And a parasol of crinkled crepe with a flowered handle."

"But the gown doesn't suit me."

Libby's hands stilled on the tiny buttons running up her back. "Doesn't suit you? Are you blind, girl? It suits you perfectly. You shall take it and that is that."

Well, the rest of her life was out of her control. Her wardrobe might as well be, also, Constance thought.

Before Libby was through, Constance had also acquired an outing suit of dark blue serge lined with gray silk, which extended out over the revers on the collar of the Eton jacket.

Matching gray satin in flat piping was stitched in rows around
the bottom of the skirt. Libby contended it was a bit too mod-
erate a style between a flat and a fluff, but Constance claimed
it a compromise. To complete the outfit, Libby selected a straw
sailor hat with a broad navy ribbon about the crown.

Libby agreed to a simple gray tailored skirt and white shirt
front with a French lawn tie. "Terribly popular this season."
A swivelled gingham gown of rich green was Constance's favorite purchase. It looked like a soft silk poplin, and enhanced
her eyes as no other gown she'd ever owned.

Outside Libby's shop, Constance paused with the children
beside her. Did she dare take time to stop at Pierce's General
Store? *Why not?* Justin had said they were to meet him at the
bank, but hadn't set a time.

She'd forgotten the extent of variety in a general store. It
had been years since she'd been inside one, what with all the
specialty shops today. The comforting smell of leather from
shoes, saddles, and harnesses mingled with the pungent odor
of kerosene. Both odors dwindled as she neared the counter,
replaced by the smell of vinegar in the pickle barrel she passed,
and the more subtle scents of lavender and rose from colognes
and soaps.

Impulsively, she selected a bottle of lavender scent and a box
of matching powder. Perhaps if she eliminated Marian's lily-
of-the-valley claim on her bedchamber, her guilt would lessen
somewhat while in that room.

Effie and Evan passed up the small display of tin toys, dolls,
and board games for the candy display in front of the counter.
While they studiously considered their choices, Constance
looked through the school supplies nearby and studied the
woman wrapping a fold of red-flowered cotton in brown paper. *Could she be Mrs. Pierce?*

The woman was as slender as Aunt Libby, but was shorter
and appeared to lack the milliner's strength. Her hair was
skinned back unfashionably into a plain bun, with no curls to

soften the bony face. Her eyes were like wells of perpetual sorrow.

Undoubtedly the man working among the barrels at the back of the store was Rasmus' father. They had the same long, lean face and pointed chin. But instead of swaggering conceit, this man's face was filled with anger. His tense, thin shoulders rode permanently up beneath his ears.

"May I help you, ma'am?" the woman behind the counter asked as her customer turned away.

Constance rested her folded, gloved hands on the counter and gave the clerk her most friendly smile. "Yes, please. The children will be entering the first grade level, and will need items for school. Perhaps you could advise me?"

It was a practical purchase, she assured herself. Whether the children remained in River's Edge or returned to Chicago, they would need school supplies.

The clerk joined her at a display, Effie and Evan close behind, eager to discover what they might need for their new experience. From the variety of pencil boxes the old woman showed them, Evan selected a simple maple box. Effie preferred one in the shape of a closed parasol, with a silk tassel. Both contained a pen, a holder, lead and slate pencils, chalk, a ruler, an eraser, and a sponge.

The clerk added a small slate and a book strap for each child. "That should hold them until their teacher advises them further. The total will be $1.20."

"I'm purchasing these, also." Constance indicated the containers of lavender scent. "Would you like to select some candy, children?" She hadn't discovered nearly enough about the Pierces to leave yet.

She didn't have to ask the twins twice.

"They are fine-looking children." The woman's gaunt features softened slightly as her sad eyes rested on the whispering, pointing children.

"Thank you. They are my brother's children. Excuse me

for being so forward, but I noticed the name of the store is Pierce's General Store. Would you happen to be Mrs. Pierce?"

She nodded shortly, eyeing her warily.

"I'm pleased to meet you. I'm sure I'll frequent your establishment. You see, I'm newly married. My husband and I only arrived in town last evening." She lowered her lashes and traced a black-gloved fingertip along the raised edge of the oak counter, hoping she appeared properly nervous as a new bride. "I'm certain I'll be needing many items once we've become established."

"Have you married a local man?" Neither voice or face indicated sincere interest; the question was merely polite.

Constance pretended not to notice the lack of interest and gushed, "Mr. Justin Knight."

The woman's gaze jerked to her. *Was she surprised because Justin had been engaged to Marian, or because she hadn't expected to see the woman her son had forced to marry standing in her store?*

Bony hands slid down the woman's white apron. "I hope you'll be happy."

Constance's murmured "thank you" was lost in the slam of a door at the back of the store. She followed Mrs. Pierce's gaze to her husband and a man who appeared to be a farmer, talking in low voices behind the barrels.

The farmer looked up and tipped his wide-brimmed hat to Mrs. Pierce. She nodded at him briskly. "Good day, Mr. Meeker."

The children placed their selections on the counter, Evan a striped peppermint stick and Effie a gracefully curved piece of ruby ribbon candy, and Mrs. Pierce collected Constance's money with shaking fingers. The woman's attention was no longer on Constance and the twins, but wandered constantly to the two men. *What disturbed Mrs. Pierce so about the farmer?*

When Constance turned at the door, she noticed Mrs. Pierce hurrying toward the two men, her new customers forgotten.

That evening for dinner, Constance wore the new green gown. The admiration in Mr. Knight's eyes when he saw her in it took her breath. Each time their gazes met across the perfectly appointed table, she was so aware of him that she'd lose her train of thought. She couldn't recall when the look in a man's eyes had caused her to feel so flustered.

To her delight, Justin had asked Libby to join them for dinner. The older woman's presence gave the meal almost a party atmosphere, and lightened the tension between the newly married couple.

The only pall on Constance's evening was the continual reminder of Marian's broken engagement, by the use of the exquisite crystal, china, and silver she had selected.

They were almost through dessert when the robbery came up in conversation. Quite natural that it should, since it was the most popular topic in town, next to Justin and Constance's wedding. When Libby mentioned the robbery, Justin dismissed the children from the table, and Constance was glad of his concern for them.

"To think that one of River's Edge's own boys should come to this!" Libby puffed like a tugboat at the thought. "Rasmus Pierce always was a troublesome youngster, but never in my wildest dreams would I have believed he would become a thief!"

"Does he appear freely among the townspeople?"

Justin's brow furrowed at Constance's query. "What makes you ask?"

"I thought perhaps with his parents living in River's Edge and having been raised here, the townspeople might tend to look aside if he visited his family or friends."

"Hmpf!" Libby's flat chest heaved in indignation. "As though a man such as that would have friends!"

"I shouldn't be surprised if he visited his parents," Justin offered, "though I've never seen him do so or heard anyone mention seeing him. Not since his chosen vocation became known."

Libby sighed dramatically. "My heart goes out to his poor, sweet mother."

"Yes," Constance agreed. "I've always felt that parents would be shamed by their children's criminal behavior."

Libby lowered her crystal water goblet and shook her head until her tight gray curls wobbled. "I don't believe it's shame Mrs. Pierce feels over Rasmus. It's sadness, pure and deep and simple. Sadness, because her son has made choices that can't bring happiness to his life, and that bring unhappiness to others."

A knock at the front door interrupted the discussion. Mrs. Kelly hurried out of the room where she'd begun to clear the table. A moment later she was back. "There's a man to see ye, Mr. Knight. A stranger, he be, by the name of Alexander Bixby."

Alexander Bixby! Constance hoped her face didn't reveal her shock.

Had the Superintendent assigned Alexander to the train robbery case? She wasn't aware of a contract between the Pinkerton Agency and the Chicago, Milwaukee and St. Paul Railroad, but it was common for railroad and express companies to hire the Pinkerton agency for such cases.

Her heart was beating faster than a steam engine at full throttle. *What will Alexander think, finding me married to another man?*

six

Constance could barely keep her attention on her conversation with Aunt Libby. *What are Alexander and Justin discussing?* At Justin's instructions, Mrs. Kelly had taken Alex directly to the library. He and Justin had been there ten minutes already, and Alexander didn't even know she was in the house.

"Aunt Libby. . ."

Constance started as Justin spoke from beside her. He stopped in front of Libby, giving her his wonderful smile.

"The man in the library is a Pinkerton agent, here to discuss the train robbery. Since Constance and I were on the train at the time, he would like to speak with both of us. I do hope you will forgive the extreme breach of etiquette if we speak with him?"

At the word "Pinkerton" Libby had clasped both hands to her lace-covered chest and drawn a breath so deep that Constance was sure it threatened to break her stays.

"A Pinkerton agent! How thrilling! But what does he think you can possibly know about the robbery?"

"I'm sure he's speaking with everyone he can locate who was on the train. Doubtless he will find our account unenlightening. I know I needn't tell you that he doesn't wish his visit known. You're much too wise to spread confidential information."

"Why, of course I'll not divulge it! I'll just take my leave. You needn't see me to the door. I'm only family."

"I knew we could count on you to understand. I've asked Mrs. Kelly to have the stable boy harness the carriage and see you home. Come, Constance."

Alexander was examining some of Justin's library volumes when they entered. She knew from his position that the books he was looking at were the Pinkerton volumes, and she couldn't help but smile.

"Mr. Bixby."

At Justin's voice, Alexander swung to face them, his hands clasped loosely behind his back. "Allow me to introduce my wife. Constance, this is Alexander Bixby of the Pinkerton Agency."

Alexander's eyes peered at her, like glittering pieces of onyx, from deep beneath his brows. His face paled so it almost rivaled the white collar of the shirt beneath his gray suit, his black hair and mustache not enhancing his color. If the situation were not so serious, Constance would have laughed. *Alexander, the star performer of their Pinkerton division, speechless*, she mused.

Before either she or Alexander could respond to Justin's introduction, Effie came tearing into the room like a miniature whirlwind, with Evan close at her heels. She swung against Constance's skirt, her feet pushing the Brussels carpet into a ridge as she skidded to a stop.

"Have you and Justin decided if we can sleep in the Bird Cage tonight?"

Constance steadied her with gentle hands on the girl's shoulders. "You mustn't. . ."

"Alex!"

At Evan's exclamation, Effie spun toward the guest. "Alex!"

This time it was Effie following Evan across the room. Each of the children chose one of Alex's trousered legs to lean against while bombarding him with questions. "When did you get here?"

"Are you going to live here, too?"

"We came on a train!"

"Bad men came on the train, but we weren't scared!"

"Are you goin' to marry Aunt Constance now?"

"Silly! He can't marry her. She's married to Mr. Knight."

Justin's gaze, filled with questions, met hers.

Why did she feel so defensive, as though she should have told him about Alexander earlier? She'd had no reason to think the two men would ever meet.

"Alex, Mr. Bixby, was my brother's good friend. When Mrs. Kelly announced him, I had no idea he was the same man we knew back in Chicago."

He didn't look convinced, yet there could be no doubting that the children knew Alex well. She hurried toward them. "Alexander is here to discuss business with Mr. Knight. I think you should go to your room and dress for bed."

"But we want to see Alex!" Evan protested.

"Can we show him the Bird cage?"

"Perhaps another time, Effie." Constance held out her hands to the children. "I'm sure after coming all this way from Chicago, Alexander wouldn't leave River's Edge without seeing you."

"Not a chance of it!" Alex squatted down. "Do I get a hug before you run upstairs?"

Effie threw her arms around his neck, but Evan stepped back and held out his hand. "Boys don't give hugs," he informed earnestly.

"Can we sleep in the Bird Cage?" Effie asked again, turning from Alex.

"May we. Yes. I've already requested Mrs. Kelly place bedding out for you."

"Thank you, Aunt Constance! C'mon, Evan!"

The children raced from the room. Their feet thudding against the marble hallway and then up the stairs kept the adults abreast of their path. Once the sounds died away, Alexander began questioning Justin and Constance concerning the robbery. Neither Alexander or Constance revealed her association with the Pinkerton agency.

Seated at one end of the leather sofa, Constance kept her

gaze on Alexander. He was as professional as always. What did he think of her marriage to Justin Knight? The color that had fled when Justin introduced her was back in his strong, lean face with its high cheekbones beneath shiny black hair.

When Mrs. Kelly came to the door to make a request of Justin, Alexander took the opportunity to whisper to Constance, "Meet me at the stable out back at midnight."

Minutes later, Alexander took his leave.

Constance started for the stairway. "I'd best check on the children."

"Mrs. Kelly is with them. I'd like to speak with you before we retire."

Reluctantly, she re-entered the library. Taking a deep breath, she turned to face him. Might as well put the discussion behind her.

He leaned back against his desk and crossed his arms. The mellow light from the lamp beside him didn't reach his face, and the shadows made his eyes seem dark and unfathomable. "Is Mr. Bixby your friend as well as your brother's?"

"Yes. We met through Charles."

"Evan asked Bixby whether he was planning to marry you. Yet when I asked last night whether you were engaged to anyone, you said no."

"I am not engaged to Mr. Bixby, or to anyone else."

"But he's in love with you?"

She felt the color rise to her cheeks at his impertinent question. "I cannot answer as to the state of another's heart."

"Has he asked you to marry him?"

"Does it matter?"

The silence after she snapped the question seemed to last an hour, though the monotonous ticking of the mahogany-encased clock on the desk counted off less than a minute before Justin answered.

"Forgive me. I have no right to pursue this."

His willingness to retreat destroyed her stubborn attitude. "It is I who should beg your forgiveness for being snappish. Your engagement is broken because of our marriage. It's only fair you know about Alexander."

She turned away from him, crossing toward the fireplace with its wide mantle at the end of the room.

"Alexander did ask me to marry him after Charles died. The children love him, as you could plainly see this evening. He would have taken them into his home if we married, and raised them gladly."

"You turned down his offer?"

She nodded. "As you know, he is a Pinkerton operative. That is a dangerous life. He would hate to leave the agency or pursue a less adventurous career. And I would hate for the children to lose a second father."

"So you refused him for the children's sake, and for his own?"

She turned to face him across the room, her hands linked lightly behind her back, but didn't reply.

"I wonder if you could have refused him so nobly if you were in love with him."

Indignation flooded her chest, and her nails bit into the flesh of her palms. She fought to keep her voice calm.

"You walked away from your own marriage plans to protect the twins. Do you think you are the only person capable of honorable actions?"

He crossed the room, stopping only inches from her. She forced herself not to retreat, though she quivered inside at his nearness. His eyes studied hers until she felt he'd taken her heart out and examined it. When he finally spoke, his voice was low.

"No, I don't think I'm the only person capable of honorable actions. But I believe if you loved a man, you would not be such a weak creature that you would refuse him out of fear that he might die on you."

She turned sharply away. How could he think he knew her so well after such a short time?

"Mr. Bixby seems like a fine man, but I think I pity him."

Pitied Alex? "Because of me?"

"Because of the profession he's chosen."

Constance whirled about in surprise. "But he loves his profession! And he's very accomplished at it."

"I'm sure he is. But I've read Allan Pinkerton's accounts of some of the cases his agency has handled." He waved a hand toward the bookcases holding the volumes Alexander had been examining when they entered the library earlier. The light danced off the gold lettering on their maroon leather bindings. "Sometimes the detectives. . ."

"Operatives."

"Pardon?"

She flushed. "Alex says Pinkerton agents are not to refer to themselves as detectives, as the title has negative connotations. Agents are called operatives."

"I see. Sometimes operatives are required to perform unsavory acts to capture criminals."

"If you've read Mr. Pinkerton's works, you are aware that he believed the ends justify the means." She flashed him a smile. "You see, I have read the volumes, also. Don't you agree with his philosophy?"

"I most decidedly do not. Without limits, it's difficult to tell where the line is that separates justice and injustice. How does your friend Mr. Bixby know when, or if, he has crossed that line?"

"I assure you Mr. Bixby is a fine, upstanding young man. His morals are unimpeachable."

"No man is so perfect that he can rely solely upon his own instincts of right or wrong. We must have a guide if mass confusion is not to reign on the earth."

"And upon what do you believe one should rely to make such judgments?"

"The Bible, the Word of God."

She should have realized that would be his solution. "You think the book infallible? Much injustice has been committed over the years in the name of God."

"Unfortunately, that is true. Still, man has trusted the Book through centuries. I would rather rely on it than myself, knowing how easily a man's judgment can be swayed by his emotions."

Seated at the desk in her room later, she paused in writing her day's report for the agency to reflect on Justin's words. From the time she first began hearing of Allan Pinkerton's work and the good he'd done in the name of justice, he'd been the nearest thing to a hero in her life. She'd believed in him so strongly that she'd never questioned his belief system. "The ends justify the means" was a basic tenet in his philosophy.

He would likely have given little weight to anything Justin Knight had to say. Mr. Pinkerton was an atheist, and had no qualms in admitting it. She'd embraced his thoughts on religion as eagerly as she had on other topics.

She had told Justin that the Bible was not infallible. Neither was Mr. Allan Pinkerton, she had to admit.

Justin's face with his steady eyes drifted across her mind. He'd sacrificed much for her and the children. He was an intelligent, honorable man even though a Christian. Or perhaps *because* he was a Christian? She didn't like the way his faith made her feel the inadequacy of her own standards of right and wrong, and set the stirrings of doubt threatening her own system of beliefs and ideals.

With a sigh, she returned to her writing. The faint scent of lavender she'd dabbed on her wrists earlier drifted to her as she signed the personalized stationery upon which she'd penned the report. Guilt pulled another string in her heart at the sight of the delicate golden script at the top of the linen page which indicated the sender was Mrs. Justin Knight. She should have found other stationery upon which to pen the report. Hadn't she appropriated enough of the items Marian had selected to use as Justin's wife?

She folded the note and placed it in an envelope, then rose impatiently. She hadn't felt as much guilt in years as she had since that disgusting marriage ceremony less than two days earlier. *What a useless emotion!* She wouldn't allow herself to become so maudlin again.

The bong of the grandfather clock in the lower floor hallway solemnly and unhurriedly announced the midnight hour. She plucked a paisley shawl from the chaise lounge at the end of the bed and pulled it over the shoulders of her green gown.

It seemed providence that the children were sleeping on the third floor of the tower. Justin had thoughtfully offered to sleep in the room off the Bird Cage in order to be close by if the children needed something or became frightened during the night; so like him to do so. She wouldn't need to worry at awakening any of them as she stole out to meet Alexander.

She didn't like that word 'stole.'

There she went again, allowing her Justin Knight-influenced conscience to prick at her, and when she'd determined not to let guilt muddy her heart or mind!

The moon was full, the cloudless sky studded with stars that watched as she hurried across the lawn. It was a good thing the tower was in the front of the house. No chance of Justin seeing her in this bright moonlight.

The door of the stable stood slightly ajar. Was Alexander already there, awaiting her? She slid into the darkness. Fresh hay, oats, leather, and less pleasant, more pungent odors, surrounded her. *Was that the sound of mice scurrying in the hay, or was it Alex moving about?*

"Alexander?"

"Here." He touched her sleeve a moment after answering her in a whisper no louder than her own. "Let's stay by the door where there's a little moonlight, and fresh air. Why did I say I'd meet you here rather than the carriage house?"

She could hear the laugh in his last statement. One of the horses snorted, and the hoofs of another thudded lightly against straw-covered floorboards. The stable may be more odorous than the carriage house, but the sounds would help cover their voices.

Her eyes were growing accustomed to the darkness, and in the faint light of moonbeams, through the door which stood slightly ajar, she made out Alexander's face, the mustache a black shadow beneath his straight nose. His eyebrows were like a small ledge above two caves that were his eyes.

His hand remained on her arm. It tightened slightly now. "Are you all right?" His voice was hoarse with anxiety.

"Yes."

"Thank God! When I heard you'd been forced into a marriage with a complete stranger. . . ." His broad shoulders drooped slightly beneath the gray coat that looked black in the moonlight. "Thought I'd lose my mind for worry over you." He cleared his throat. "Came up to the house immediately upon arriving by train tonight. Couldn't wait to make certain no harm had come to you, or the children."

His concern was heartwarming. "We're all fine, as you saw for yourself."

"Knight hasn't made any, demands on you?"

"Alexander!" Even in the darkness she knew her cheeks flamed at his question, and she tugged her arm from his hold. "Justin Knight is a gentleman, in every sense of the word."

"I'm sorry if I offended you by asking, but you never know what kind of bounder. . . ." He caught her about the waist and pulled her close. "I should have married you back in Chicago. Should have ignored your excuses. Then you and the children wouldn't be in this mess. But I knew how important it was for you to continue as an operative, and didn't press my attentions."

She pushed against his chest with both hands until he released her. "I shall excuse your behavior this evening due to the trying circumstances. But I have never given you permission to touch me in such an intimate manner, and I expect that you shall not do so again!"

"You know I love you, that I. . ."

"Please, Alexander!" She wanted to shout at him instead of whisper. "It is all I can do to keep fear for the children aside and act professionally in the present situation. Please do not ask me to assume the added emotional distress of another proposal at this time."

"As you wish." His voice was tight with anger. She knew if the light were brighter, she would see that his lips were tight also. "You haven't told Knight that you're an operative?"

"Of course not! Have I ever revealed my position to anyone without the Superintendent's approval?"

"Sorry. Had to be sure."

"What. . .what did the superintendent say about the marriage?"

"He thinks it's marvelous. Thinks your position as a prominent banker's wife may serve the agency's purposes well." Bitterness all but rattled his teeth. "Didn't seem concerned that Knight might be a rounder, that you might be endangered living in the man's home. Said that of course an annulment would be obtained when Pierce was apprehended."

Should she tell him that Justin was against an annulment? *No.* Even in the darkness, anger shouted from the tense manner in which he held himself. She handed him her envelope.

"Here is my daily report. I suppose you'll wish to read it, since you're on the case now. When you have, would you post it for me?"

He stuffed it into an inside coat pocket. "Sure. Might as well bring you up to date on the case. From what you and Knight said earlier, you're already aware Rasmus Pierce and his mob pulled the strike on the train."

"I almost forgot to tell you! I posted the information in my report last night but," she stepped closer in her eagerness, "Rasmus doesn't look anything like the image on his Bertillon card. He's grown his hair and wears it rather like Buffalo Bill Cody, back behind his ears, though his is limp and stringy instead of full and curly like that famous man's. And he has a Vandyke beard."

"You're certain it's Rasmus and not another member of the mob you're describing?"

"I'm certain. It was he who insisted on the marriage. He threatened to harm Effie and Evan if we didn't agree to the ceremony."

"You shudder like that again and I'll forget my resolve to be the gentleman you requested."

She stepped back hurriedly with a slight gasp.

"You needn't be afraid of me." The pain beneath the anger in his tone caused her to regret her actions immediately.

Before she could apologize, he switched the subject. "No wonder you went along with the marriage, if the children were threatened. It's going to be a real pleasure putting that bounder behind bars." His thick eyebrows met. "Think I'll check out that minister. Haven't spoken to him yet. Maybe there's a chance he's not legitimate."

"Justin says the man serves a church in Red Wing. But, of course, it would be good to verify that." Not that she believed for a moment that Justin would lie, not honorable Justin. But her experience with the agency had taught her that no one is to be completely trusted. "What else have you learned of the robbery?"

He gave her a quick report, but revealed nothing she didn't already know, with the exception of the listing of other agents who were joining him in the area. Most were going to be in disguise, working at menial positions about town where they could be available if needed, and where they might pick up information from local gossip or observation. He was to be the agent in charge.

When he'd revealed all, he poked his head cautiously through the door to glance about. "All clear. Better let you out of here before you begin smelling like a stable hand. That would prick Knight's curiosity!"

But she didn't leave.

"Alex, do you ever wonder about the morality of the deception we use as operatives?"

He scowled and shrugged. "It's necessary. You know that." Impatience tinged his voice. "Can't expect to walk up to a criminal and say 'by your leave, I'd like to arrest you. Would you be so kind as to give testimony against yourself?'"

She smiled at the scene he portrayed.

"What brought on this attack of conscience?"

"I was thinking of the danger to which I've exposed the children, and. . ." she shrugged slightly.

"Charles was my closest friend. The twins' safety is important to me, too."

"I know. I'll not allow sentimentality to sway my good sense again."

She'd just started through the door when he detained her with a hand on her shoulder.

"You know where I'm staying, Constance. I'll be keeping as close a watch as possible on you. If anything changes, if you should find the situation with Knight. . .I'm here if you need me."

She covered his hand with her own; released it after a quick squeeze. "Thank you." She was tempted to tell him that in spite of her earlier actions, she liked him very much. She'd best not. It would be cruel to encourage him unless she knew she loved him, especially as she was presently married, temporarily, to Justin.

When had she begun thinking of him as Justin instead of Mr. Knight? she wondered, hurrying across the new lawn. The spicy scent of the bright yellow and amber chrysanthemums in the plaster urns beside the back walk hung thickly in the air.

She wished the Superintendent wasn't so enthusiastic about her position as Mrs. Justin Knight. It was clear from Alexander's comments that the Superintendent expected her to keep her position with the agency a secret. She'd been hoping to be allowed to tell Justin the truth.

In the past, she'd been proud of her ability to deceive. It was that which made her such a valuable operative, after all. But it disturbed her more every passing hour to deceive Justin. She'd never met a man who held honesty in such high esteem. She'd like to have his respect. What would he think when he discovered she was an operative? If only he believed that the ends justified the means, she wouldn't worry so that he would despise her when the truth was revealed.

seven

Attending church had never been such a trying experience.

After Charles's death, Constance had attended faithfully, knowing it was important to him that his children be raised in the church. Usually, she allowed her mind to drift during the sermons, and afterward enjoyed pleasant visits with friends and neighbors. It was a friendly, comfortable place to be in spite of her lack of faith.

Today was different. The congregation's eyes were on her and Justin more than on the pastor. Certainly few people in attendance paid any attention whatever to the sermon.

Constance, however, couldn't avoid listening to the sermon. Its theme was the same verse the minister had quoted on the train: "All things work together for good to them that love God." *Was it a coincidence?* Surely the pastor couldn't have chosen the verse because of her and Justin; he wasn't aware that they hadn't married of their own free will. *Was the verse true?* A longing to believe it tugged at Constance. It would be comforting to have such a promise to grasp in a world where terrible things happen to people and evil often appeared to triumph.

During the closing prayer, she spread the palm of her left hand over the skirt of her filmy yellow organdy. Her wedding band raised a small lump beneath her pale yellow glove. The ring should have been presented to Marian this afternoon. The thought made her cringe.

The benediction over, the congregation rose to leave.

"Think you can play the part of the happy bride?" Justin whispered beneath the brim of her flowered leghorn before turning to Effie and Evan.

Could she play the part? If only he knew the extent of her experience as an actress mastering all manner of roles for the agency. When he turned back again, she slipped her hand beneath his arm and smiled so rapturously up at him that he blinked in astonishment.

The fun died in her when, walking down the aisle, her gaze met Marian's. The girl's blue eyes were shooting sparks above pale cheeks.

Guilt and sympathy flooded Constance, and it was all she could do to keep smiling as they swept past Marian's pew. As if the girl hadn't been humiliated and hurt enough!

And she, Constance Ward. . .uh, Knight, was taking part in causing another human being such pain. She hated herself for it.

But I have no choice!

Once outside in the early September sunshine, a few of the men tipped their hats and greeted Justin, only to be tugged hurriedly away by frowning wives. Other than the pastor and his wife, only a handful of bachelors were brave enough to offer their felicitations.

The congregation had mostly dispersed when a middle-aged man, his slender face twisted in red fury beneath his hat, fists clenched, stepped from beside a fringed buggy.

Justin touched his wide Boston derby and nodded slightly. "Mr. Ames."

Marian's father! She should have known. Would he create a scene?

"Knight, I once considered you one of the finest men I ever had the privilege of knowing. But you're nothing but a disgusting, cheap, smelly old skunk."

Before Constance realized his intentions, the wiry man flung a fist at Justin's face. It landed with a disgusting crunch on Justin's nose, and she felt him stagger against her.

Dropping her parasol, she grabbed Justin's arm just as a second blow struck his chin, toppling him backward to the ground. Her hold on his arm carried her with him.

She was barely aware of Evan and Effie's raised voices, or the few remaining members of the congregation who stood in stunned silence. All she noticed was the blood streaming from Justin's nose as he struggled to a sitting position and helped her do the same.

"Get up and I'll give you more of the same!"

Surely the older man didn't expect Justin to actually fight him? He would be no match for Justin's youth, she had time to think before Effie flung herself against the man's leg. One little foot flashed from beneath her ivory organdy skirt in a series of wildly aimed blows, occasionally landing on Mr. Ames' shins.

"You mean old man! Don't you dare hit Justin! Don't you dare!"

"Effie! Stop this instant!" Justin fairly roared.

Effie spun and faced him. "But he. . ."

"That's enough, Effie."

The girl's eyes flashed fire. She dropped to her knees beside Evan, who was trying to stuff his handkerchief beneath Justin's nose.

Justin remained where he was, knees drawn up, one hand taking the kerchief from Evan. "I know what I did to your daughter is as close to unforgivable as a man's actions can come. I cannot justify myself to you or Marian. I can only say that I am sincerely sorry for any harm, "

"Sorry!" The man turned his head and spat. "*That* for your apology. You aren't worthy of a woman like Marian. Good thing she discovered in time what a rotter you are. Just see your bank try to stay afloat in these hard times now that the entire town knows how little stock they can put in your word."

He strode to the buggy, still shaking in anger. Marian was

waiting for him there, a triumphant smile on her beautiful face.

What must Justin be feeling, Constance wondered with a pang, to be publicly attacked before the girl he loved?

When the buggy was clattering down the street, Justin slipped a hand beneath Constance's elbow. "Have you been hurt?"

"No. But your nose."

"I've had bloodied noses before. Of course, the last time it was over a baseball, and I was the ripe old age of ten."

Her concern fled in a grin at his words and the twinkle in his eyes. She reached to straighten his red satin tie, which had pulled from his vest and twisted beneath the pointed wings of his high linen collar.

"I could grow accustomed to your smile, Mrs. Knight." His low, ardent tone made the words as intimate as a caress. She stared at him, incredulous, lips slightly parted, her fingers frozen at his vest.

He turned to Effie and Evan a moment later, and she was glad of the opportunity to recover her composure.

"Thanks for the handkerchief, old man."

Effie propped her fists on her hips, her mouth screwed into a pout. "Why didn't you hit him back?"

He pushed a curl behind her ear. "Remember the talk we had the first night in our new house? We should always do what we think Jesus would do. I didn't think Jesus would hit Mr. Ames."

"I suppose we better pray for him, too." Evan sighed resignedly. "Like that mean old Rasmus."

Justin grinned, pushing himself from the ground. "You've got the right idea, Evan." He bent to assist Constance to her feet.

Effie crossed her arms over her lace-covered chest and snorted. "Pretty soon we're going to have so many people to pray for that we won't have time to do anything else."

"Life could hold worse possibilities," Justin replied, grinning, and handed Constance her parasol. His gaze fell to her skirt. "I'm afraid your gown has been ruined. There's both a grass stain and a tear."

"It's only a dress." She tried to keep the disappointment out of her voice. She'd felt positively frivolous in the gown at first, after months of black gowns and mourning hats, but she truly liked it.

"I'll buy you another."

"That isn't. . ."

"You look like sunshine in it."

Her heart skipped a beat. She had to lower her gaze from his to allow herself to catch her breath. What had beset the man that he was making such boldly personal comments?

"Perhaps it can be repaired. I'll speak with Aunt Libby about it Monday morning."

They began walking the five blocks to the house. The children ran on ahead, clambering over every horse stoop, and balancing along the tops of occasional stone fences, with Effie leading the way as usual.

"I. . . I. . . there is something I should like to say."

His smile could have chased away clouds. "Is it so serious you must pucker those lovely eyebrows into a frown?"

"This entire situation is serious!"

"But not tragic, I hope. What is the problem?"

"It's only. . . I. . . it's your wedding day. Or it was meant to be. It shall likely be especially difficult for you to have the children and me in your home today instead of Miss Marian. If you'd like, I shall take the children to Aunt Libby's for the afternoon."

His smile faded somewhat, but didn't disappear altogether.

"You are most thoughtful, but that won't be necessary. I'd much prefer your company to your absence."

Did he hope their company would help divert his thoughts? *He is such a kind man. If only he could have been spared this heartbreak.*

It must be awful for him, unable to explain the situation, allowing people to believe he has gone back on his word, Constance thought. *The townspeople should know him better than to believe the worst.* Why she'd only known him two days and she already knew he would never renege on his word unless it was impossible to keep it.

What was happening to her good sense? She knew better than to trust anyone.

Justin drew her hand through his arm solicitously. "Is anything wrong? I thought I heard you gasp."

She denied it with a quick shake of her head, disturbingly conscious of his touch.

Constance gave up trying to argue with her detective training and allowed herself to enjoy the rest of the walk home, well aware that the newlyweds made an interesting spectacle for the neighborhood: Justin with a bloodied nose and herself in a torn, stained gown.

Her brother would have liked Justin. Not only because the man shared her brother's faith, but because he lived it.

She was accustomed to men with high morals. It was required of Pinkerton agents that they not have addiction to vices such as drinking, smoking, card playing, or low dives, and that they be of "a high order of mind."

Yet, she didn't know another man, including Charles, who would have had the strength of character not to at least retaliate in words when Mr. Ames struck him. He forgave Rasmus, forgave Mr. Ames, and kept silent about the cause of their marriage to his own detriment in order to protect the children. Not only the character of every other man she'd known, but her own character as well, seemed weak by comparison.

The front door slammed behind the twins, rattling the lovely etched glass. Constance and Justin were halfway up the front walk before it opened again and Effie stuck her head out, brown curls bobbing.

"Hurry! There's a present on the dining room table."

"Oh, dear," Constance said, entering the door Justin held for her. "That reminds me. What of the wedding gifts you and Marian received?"

"They were displayed at Marian's house. I assume she will see to returning them."

The nightmare never seemed to end for Marian.

A large package wrapped in beautiful mauve paper sat in the middle of the linen cloth covering the dining room table. She reached for the card, then dropped it as though it were on fire.

"Rasmus!"

eight

Justin grabbed the card. "'Best wishes to the Bride and Groom. Fondly, Rasmus.'" In a quick, fierce gesture, he crumpled the card in one hand. "How dare he intrude in my house, threaten my family!" The balled-up card bounced against the tiny, cheerful gold print of the wallpaper on the opposite wall and fell upon the red, cream, and gold carpet.

My family. The words echoed through Constance's mind, even as she grasped the edge of the table with her yellow gloves.

"He's showing us that he meant what he said, isn't he? That he can easily reach and harm the children if he chooses."

"I'm afraid so, yes." The words were tight, furious.

She turned and darted for the door, grasping her pale yellow skirts. "The Bird Cage! If he departed within the last few minutes, perhaps we can see him from there!"

He was past her in an instant, taking the steps two at a time, coattails flying.

When she reached the open tower room, his hands were resting on the wide railing. She knew without asking that he hadn't seen Rasmus. Disappointment was in the sag of his shoulders, the dejected line of his lips. Still, she rushed to one of the openings to search for herself, snatching up Justin's eyeglass, making her gaze stop at every movement until convinced Rasmus was nowhere in sight.

"I expect he came during the church service, Constance. He'd know we have no live-in servants, that the day servants would be at their own homes on Sunday and there'd be no one to see him enter."

Suddenly lightheaded and nauseous, she leaned against the

balustrade surrounding the tower room. She could taste fear on her tongue, feel it in the rage in her chest. The children— she could hear their laughter from the open window of their bedchamber below—to think anyone would be so vile as to threaten them.

The Justin was gently urging her head against his shoulder. It was so comforting in his arms. Too comforting.

She pushed herself away, instantly missing his strength.

He caught her elbows lightly, but didn't try to draw her back into his embrace. She stared at his gold scarf pin, avoiding the disturbing intensity of his eyes. "I've never known a woman with your strength. But you needn't be strong every moment. I'm going to be beside you, sharing your burden for the children until Rasmus is behind bars."

His fervent promise almost crumbled the weak defenses she'd built against her attraction to him. She didn't doubt the sincerity of his concern for the children, but she mustn't forget he loved Marian.

"Rasmus is only trying to keep us frightened, Constance. If we continue to do as he requested, he has no reason to harm Effie and Evan."

She took a deep breath and met his gaze.

"Perhaps we should contact Alex, Mr. Bixby. He may wish to speak with the neighbors, to see whether anyone saw Rasmus."

His mouth tightened slightly. "I'll try to catch him at his hotel."

While he was gone, she changed from her torn frock into her new white shirtwaist, navy silk tie, and gray skirt. She worried every moment he was away. The house was so huge. How would she know, until too late, if Rasmus returned? A dozen times she looked in on the children, assuring herself they were safe.

When she heard the front door, Constance rushed for the hallway. Relief flooded her at the sight of Justin and Alex.

Justin was hanging his pale gray Boston derby on the walnut and brass hat rack when he saw her. He squeezed her hands and smiled down at her, and the world seemed steady and safe again.

"Mr. Bixby and I decided to come directly back and talk here. Is the gift still in the dining room?"

"I've removed it to the library to prepare the table for luncheon." Had Justin suggested the men return here to speak because he realized how upset she was at being alone with the children?

"Then we'll be in the library if you need us." He dismissed her with a nod.

"May I join you?" She ignored Justin's raised eyebrows at her severe breach of etiquette, inviting herself to a business conference between men.

"Of course, you may." Trust Justin's gentlemanly nature to win out. His voice and manner didn't show a hint of disapproval or surprise, in spite of the shock she'd seen in his eyes a moment earlier. He took her elbow and ushered her into the library as though it were the most natural occurrence in the world.

She lowered herself onto the edge of the leather wing chair to which Justin led her, uncomfortably aware he remained standing beside her. Was he not so subtly reinforcing to Bixby that she was his wife? She dismissed the idea immediately as absurd.

"Guess you can tell for yourself, Bixby, that the fancy-wrapped box on the desk is the gift. Constance and I won't object at all if you do the honors and open it. You've already read the card."

She recognized the almost imperceptible tightening that deepened the lines at the corners of Alexander's dark eyes, warning of his displeasure. Did he think Justin's actions toward her too proprietary?

"Nothing unusual in this," he said, pulling out a pair of tall, exquisite silver candlesticks. "Expect they were purchased with stolen money."

"Your mistake. They belong to Marian's parents."

Constance couldn't contain a gasp at Justin's revelation. "You're certain?"

"I doubt there are two pair of candlesticks of that size and quality in this town. Hadn't heard the Ameses had been robbed. We'll have the dickens of a time trying to return the candlesticks. How do we explain why Rasmus would steal them, then give them to us as a gift?"

Alex shook his head. "That crook doesn't miss a trick. I'll return them for you. Don't worry, I won't let the Ames know where I discovered them. I'll just say I came across them in the investigation, and that it could damage the possibility of capturing the criminals if I reveal the details."

"Thanks, Bixby."

"I'd best get some agents started on checking out the neighborhood, see if we can locate anyone who saw Rasmus this morning." He picked up one of the candlesticks and quirked an eyebrow. "Might try the Ames's neighborhood, too."

He paused beside her. "You and the children stick close to Knight this afternoon. I'll arrange for an operative to pose as a stable and yard man, so there will be someone with you and the twins when Knight's at work. The man will be on the place by dusk."

Dusk still seemed a long way off, Constance thought at six that evening, looking out across the Mississippi from the edge of the steep limestone bluff just north of town. Behind her, Effie and Evan were chasing a butterfly across an expanse of rock-strewn meadow.

How thoughtful it was of Justin to get them out of the house. Had he realized she'd been looking around corners since they'd discovered Rasmus' gift?

She smiled at him as he lowered himself to the plaid blanket covering the large gray rock.

"It's so peaceful here. The river doesn't look like the Big Muddy today, with the waters bluer than the sky. I would never have guessed the Mississippi was this wide. I can barely see the bluffs on the opposite side. They look a hazy blue, like mountains from a distance."

He leaned against the trunk of a scraggly pine, one of many scenting the breeze, resting his forearms on his updrawn knees. He'd changed from the formal suit he'd worn for church to soft brown trousers topped by a Norfolk jacket.

"This is one of my favorite places. The pines on the craggy cliffs hide numerous caves where I played with friends as a boy." He broke a twig idly between his fingers and tossed it over the edge of the bluff. "For a time, when Rasmus and I had a questionable truce, he even joined in our escapades here."

Evan appeared suddenly, throwing his arms about Justin's neck and almost knocking him over.

"Hey, old man, practicing to be a football player?"

Giggles were his only answer. The boy lay panting on the blanket beside him as he continued. "My friends and I would pretend we were Tom Sawyer and his friends. We had quite the spine-tingling adventures. There's even a cave in these bluffs we dubbed Pirate's Cave. We pretended it contained smuggled treasure."

Evan jerked up. "Pirate's Cave?"

"It was only make-believe." Justin rumpled the brown curls. "Your sister's calling."

The boy was off to join her in a flash.

When Justin turned his attention back to Constance, his eyebrows shot up. "You're laughing at me. Why?"

"It is difficult to imagine you as a child. You seem so. . .comfortably adult."

His mouth curved down temporarily. "Old and staid, that's me. That's why I thought Marian. . ."

He didn't finish the sentence. Did he think he would insult her by speaking of his fiancee? How silly. And he certainly wasn't old and staid, with his warm brown eyes and rich laugh. Every time she looked at him, she felt his arms about her as they'd been earlier.

"Marian would bring life and energy to any home." The admission hurt.

"So do the children." She followed his gaze to them, where they played leap-frog with awkward grace.

Eventually her gaze drifted from the children to discover him watching her, two lines cutting between his brows.

"I'd thought for a time, Constance, that coming here had served the purpose I wished and relaxed you, but the tension is back in your face."

"I can't put Rasmus' threats from my mind after his visit to your home. Is there anyone more vile than a person who threatens children?"

"No!" His fists tightened into white knuckled balls. "But we shall continue to do all we can to protect them."

Constance remembered his words when he saw Rasmus' card, "How dare he threaten my family!" and a sweet longing stole through her.

She played idly with one of the blossoms amidst the pile of fragrant wildflowers, clover, and dandelions which Effie had deposited in the lap of her gray skirt for safe-keeping.

"I know you shall. Your goodness to myself and the children continually amazes me. It is myself, and Rasmus, with whom I am upset."

"Yourself?" He leaned forward earnestly, arms about his knees. "But you have done nothing for which you should be upset. On the contrary, you've acted bravely."

"If I hadn't brought the children to River's Edge, they would not have been endangered."

"But you couldn't have known that in advance."

Would he protest so vehemently if he knew she had come to gather information on Rasmus?

"Nevertheless, I feel I've failed Charles." She lifted her hands slightly and her shoulders raised the white lawncloth shirt-waist in a dainty shrug. "Six months ago I was content with my life. Then Charles died, and I acquired sole care of the children. I love them, but I've brought them into danger. Now we are trapped in the role of your family, not knowing when the charade will end. I no longer have control over any aspect of my life."

"Do any of us have control over our lives?" He asked gently. "Isn't such control merely an illusion?"

At least he didn't reiterate his refusal to consider an annulment, she thought in relief, though she'd noticed him wince when she mentioned the charade. "I suppose you mean that God is in control."

"Yes. He allows both good things and hard things to happen to us, but He makes 'all things work together for good to them that love God,' remember?"

Did she have the courage to admit what she was thinking? Not if she continued meeting his eyes, she thought. She turned her gaze out across the river, welcoming the pine and clover scented breeze that cooled her hot cheeks and fanned the tight little curls about her forehead.

"I always considered myself a morally superior person, prid-ing myself on my high standards. Until I met you, I didn't realize the inadequacy of my own goodness. Your standards shame me, they are so much higher than my own."

Shock sat plainly on his features. "I can't imagine that your standards would be lower than mine in any manner. You are one of the finest examples of gentle womanhood I have ever known."

The sincerity in his husky voice humbled her.

"Thank you for your gallant protest. But I do not attempt to make God's standards mine, as you do."

"I fail miserably numerous times daily in attempting to live up to those standards. The Bible says only God is good. We cannot judge our actions by comparing ourselves to each other. We must compare ourselves to Christ if we wish to know whether we are good. In that comparison, we all fail."

A shaky little laugh slipped out. Strange, she didn't feel like laughing.

"That makes Him sound rather like a stern schoolmaster watching for mistakes and handing out demerits."

"Jesus wiped away all our demerits when He took our sins on Himself and paid our debt with His death on the cross."

"I saw the change believing in Christ made in Charles's life. I've seen the evidence in your life, also, so strongly that I can no longer deny His existence or power."

Something glorious leaped in his eyes.

"Charles always told me that if I believed Christ was the Son of God, and had taken my sins on Himself, all I needed do was admit to Him my need for His goodness, and He would forgive me, and be with me in a close manner. Is that what you believe?"

Was it guarded hope she saw in his eyes?

"Yes. It is what I did as a boy of fifteen. The decision to follow Christ has made all the difference in my life."

She ran the tip of her tongue quickly over her suddenly dry lips. It was such a simple little thing, just a prayer, why was it so frightening, as though she were stepping off this rock into nothing but air?

"I. . .I'm not experienced with praying. Would you. . .do you think God would mind if you prayed with me?"

One of his hands covered hers. Could he feel her trembling?

"I'm certain He'd not mind, and I would be honored to do so."

"Dear Lord and Father, we thank Thee for putting within us

a longing for the good and true in life. Thank Thee for revealing to us the inadequacy of our own attempts at goodness, and our need for Thy goodness, which is given us through the sacrifice by Christ of His own life, though we are completely undeserving of it. Thank Thee for accepting my request for Thy salvation when I was just entering manhood. We humbly request Thy gift of salvation for Constance this day, and thank Thee that Thou hast promised that Thou wilt turn away no one who comes to Thee. In Jesus' name, Amen."

Was she supposed to say something to God now, too? Were there rules about talking to Him? Constance couldn't recall when she'd felt so ignorant. She peeked up at Justin through her lashes and caught him watching her with softly glowing eyes.

"Is that all?"

"Unless you would like to add something."

"No. I . . .I wouldn't know how, even if I wished to."

"God isn't as concerned with the words we use as He is with what is in our hearts. You can talk with Him whenever you wish, however you wish, and He will listen to you. Don't worry if prayer seems strange to you at first; it did to me, too. As time goes along, you'll grow more comfortable talking with Him, the same as with people with whom you develop a friendship."

Effie slipped to her knees beside her, and Constance was glad for her timely arrival. It had been unusually exhausting discussing her decision to trust in God. She was accustomed to people who ridiculed such faith, or tolerated it in polite society, only to laugh about it behind people's backs. What would Alexander say if he knew of her change of heart?

Effie flung her arms out wide. "I'm hot! I wish I could wear short pants like Evan when we play. But I made a good frog, even in my dress, didn't you think?"

Constance bounced a fingertip off Effie's snub nose. "I'm

not a very good judge of frogs. I am glad you aren't green with spots, but are a pretty little girl instead."

Where would all their lives wind up after the cruel joke fate in the form of Rasmus Pierce had played on them? For a moment panic threatened Constance's newfound peace of spirit.

"All things work together for good to them that love God," she repeated to herself. She hoped it was true.

nine

Justin leaned against the white pillar on the back porch and stole a glance at Constance, who was watching the twins with the gift from him. She was so near he could smell the delicate lavender fragrance she wore. The scent suited her, subtle, lingering in one's senses but not clinging.

The gentle light of early evening played on her hair, and he stuffed his hands hard in his pockets to keep from caressing it. He could still feel its softness against his cheek when he held her so briefly in the Bird Cage yesterday. He longed to have her in his embrace again. But more than that, he wanted the love and respect of this sweet, courageous woman.

She looked up at him with a smile in the green eyes which so fascinated him.

"You shall spoil the children with your generosity."

"They've been through some difficult times. I hope the pony will let them forget those times for a few minutes, anyway." He nodded toward them. "They appear to have taken to Zeke, in spite of that misshapen nose above his thick black mustache." The short, slender man in the bicycle hat, a collarless tan shirt, brown corduroy knickers, and suspenders was checking the harness under Evan's watchful eyes.

"Looks like he's been on the losing end of a few bouts of fisticuffs."

"Alex made a wise choice in his selection of an operative to stay on the grounds. The children have been following him about the stable and carriage house most of the day. I must say, he's been extremely patient and agreeable with them."

Justin certainly hoped he was a wise choice. Zeke Endicott

87

had been waiting when they returned from the bluffs last evening. It had relieved his mind a great deal while at the bank to know Zeke was watching out for the three people who had become so important in his life the last few days.

He'd feel better if he were watching out for them around the clock himself, but that wasn't possible. He couldn't ignore his responsibilities at the bank. Too many banks had floundered and closed their doors the last few years. Difficult growing conditions and low rates for wheat hadn't helped midwestern banks. The current silver situation threatened even more. With the northern forests overcut and the increasing use of railroads to carry logs, the local economy, largely reliant on lumber carried on the Mississippi, was teetering precariously.

No, it was no time to be neglecting his duties, even if it did send his heart to his throat to think of leaving Constance and the children each day.

He smiled broadly as Evan climbed into the tall wooden cart and took the reins. "No, Effie. A gen'leman never 'lows a lady to drive. You're the passenger this time."

"Looks like Evan is finally standing up for himself," he said to Constance.

"He is a reserved boy, but not so timid as one might think. He chooses his battles well. Those he chooses, he generally wins."

"I expect he takes after a certain aunt in that respect."

She turned from watching the children to regard him steadily, but did not take up the challenge in his comment. "Since you and Mr. Endicott are watching the children, I believe I shall take care of my correspondence."

He watched her enter the back door, moving gracefully as always. He wished she had stayed; he enjoyed her company.

Sitting on the top step, he leaned back against the huge round planter filled with geraniums, and let his gaze move back to the children taking the cart up the drive and down, the spotted pony bouncing faithfully before them.

Only four days had passed since the forced marriage ceremony. It seemed a lifetime. Already he thought of Constance and the children as his family. He wouldn't have thought it possible for one's heart to be captured so quickly and irrevocably.

Constance had been a real trooper about this marriage. They hadn't discussed the permanency of it since that first night, though he'd been tempted to do so yesterday when she spoke in passing of the time the "charade" would be past. But there really was no point in arguing about it until Rasmus was captured.

His lips tightened at the memory of his proposal. When Constance realized Rasmus' intent to harm the children if they didn't marry, the blood had drained from her round face beneath that awful black mourning hat, but her gallant spirit had risen to the occasion. Calm determination routed the fear and dismay from her emerald eyes in less time than it takes to blink. He'd half fallen in love with her at that moment. If the situation had to happen, God had placed the right woman there.

And now she'd accepted Christ. The knowledge left a glow around his heart.

Would the Lord be able to convince her that her place was now here, beside him? As a new Christian, she couldn't be expected to understand or embrace all the Bible's teachings overnight. And there was Alexander Bixby. Did Constance love him? He wasn't certain about the legalities of an annulment, should she still choose to try obtain one against his wishes. Could one be gained on the grounds that one was forced into the marriage contract under duress?

Constance, even her name implied loyalty and faithfulness. She was a woman in a million. Even if she obtained an annulment, his heart would belong to her forever. Yesterday she'd said she felt "trapped" as his wife. The memory left a burning wound inside him. Would he be able to win her love before Rasmus was apprehended?

"Great kids, aren't they?"

Justin jerked upright.

"Didn't see you come up, Bixby." Some guardian he was proving for the children and Constance!

Shadows had formed beneath Alex's eyes since yesterday afternoon, Justin noted.

"Thought I'd stop by to let you know the latest developments."

Justin glanced at the children. Zeke was still with them; they should be safe. "Let's talk in the library."

"Is Constance about?" Alex asked as they entered the booklined room. "I'd like her to join us."

Justin felt the muscles around his mouth tighten, that stupid jealousy again.

"I hate to worry her any more than necessary."

"The children are her responsibility. I should think it would worry her more not to know how the case is progressing."

"She and the children are *my* responsibility now."

"I know the details of that marriage ceremony, remember?" Justin didn't like the way Alex's eyes narrowed and his voice lowered threateningly. "Constance may be forced to live with you for now to protect the children, but if you do anything to harm her," Alex poked a blunt-edged finger toward him, emphasizing his point, "I'll tear you limb from limb. She's not your wife permanently. Don't forget it."

As if he had to be reminded that he hadn't his wife's love and commitment! The knowledge added to the anger Alex's challenge had lit.

"Is threatening innocent people part of your job?"

"I expect to marry Constance myself when this case is over." He jammed his hands into the pockets of his brown-checked sack suit. "Now that you know how the land lies, do you want to discuss the case or not?"

Regardless of his anger with Bixby, the man was right, the children were Constance's responsibility. Besides, what did he expect to accomplish by keeping the two of them apart? Did he think Constance would forget the man? Confound it, he even liked Bixby, except for his attraction to Constance. He was intelligent, easy to meet, and obviously cared about Constance and the children.

"I'll ask *my wife* to join us."

His fury continued to seethe as he went in search of her. First Rasmus entered his home and threatened his family, and now Bixby entered his home and brazenly announced his plan to marry his wife! *Whatever happened to the idea that a man's home is his castle?*

When Constance and Justin returned to the library, Bixby didn't have all that much to relate. The Ames's had been glad to receive the candlesticks back. Apparently nothing else but an ornate silver frame holding a likeness of Marian had been taken from them. The items had been taken sometime last night while the family slept. No one in either neighborhood recalled seeing Rasmus in the area.

All known abandoned buildings in and around River's Edge had been searched since the robbery, with no sign that Rasmus' gang had been inhabiting any of them. Rasmus' parents' establishment, along with their home above the store, were under constant watch. Again, there was no indication Rasmus or any of his criminal friends had been there the last couple days. Storekeepers, horse dealers, and real estate merchants were being interviewed in hopes of discovering large or unusual purchases. No leads there yet, either.

Justin rested his elbows on the desk and pyramided his fingertips together.

"So all that's been discovered so far is where Rasmus is *not* hiding?"

The slamming of the back door and Evan's high-pitched

holler interrupted Alex's reply. Justin and Constance were at the library door by the time Evan reached it. His eyes were almost as large as the round straw hat he'd been wearing earlier.

Justin caught him by the shoulders. "Whoa, old man! What's the problem?"

"Effie fell out of the cart! She made the pony go fast. The wagon hit a rock, and Effie fell out. She's sleepin', and won't wake up!"

Justin was down the hall before Evan finished. He could hear Constance racing behind him. Terror flooded him as he dashed toward the still child lying on the ground with Zeke kneeling beside her.

"She's alive, sir," Zeke assured as Justin fell to his knees beside the girl. "Out cold, though. May have a concussion."

Justin set trembling fingers alongside Effie's neck to reassure himself Zeke's words were true.

Constance dropped beside him to take Effie's limp hand with a strangled sob, her eyes large with fear. Justin longed to comfort her, but couldn't afford the luxury. He squeezed her shoulder.

"Steady, dearest. Doctor Thomas lives only a few doors down. I'll bring him."

It was almost midnight before Dr. Thomas left. Effie had two black eyes, a swollen nose, and had lost her two top front teeth. But long before the doctor left, she had regained consciousness and was fast becoming her usual bossy self. The doctor assured them her injuries looked far worse than they were.

Little comfort, Justin thought, staring glumly between the wine-colored library draperies into the black night. He'd never forgive himself for leaving the children with the cart and pony. It had only taken a moment for Zeke to turn his back and the accident to happen. For the first time, he realized the extent of the responsibility he'd assumed for the children.

"Justin?"

He turned to find Constance close behind him. She looked like an angel in the mellow light from the desk lamp. If the accident had terrified him, how much more must it have frightened her?

He opened his mouth to comfort her and instead heard himself say, "Effie could have been killed."

A hurt sound broke from her throat. She swayed toward him, opening her arms. In two steps, he had her in his embrace, burying his face in her soft, fragrant hair.

"You mustn't blame yourself, Justin. You mustn't! Zeke was with them. He couldn't prevent it, and you wouldn't have been able to, either."

The words did nothing to ease his guilt, especially accompanied as they were by the tears in her voice.

"It must have shredded your heart to see her like that."

She pushed him away just far enough to grasp his shoulders and give him an ineffectual shaking.

"You must stop accusing yourself. In a few days, the only sign of this evening's misfortune will be the lack of Effie's two front teeth, and her temporary teeth at that. Can you imagine her trying to boss Evan about with a lisp?"

Her attempt to lift his spirits caught his heart in a twinge. If anything ever happened to this brave little woman. . . . Despair flooded him. How could he prevent it? He hadn't even been able to keep Effie from harm with a pony and cart. He swallowed the lump of anguish in his throat.

"I'll sell the pony tomorrow."

"We cannot protect the children from every possible harm. Wouldn't it be better to teach them how to act wisely around the pony?"

He recognized the wisdom of her words, but he couldn't stop wishing he could protect Effie and Evan always.

One of her hands slipped tentatively from his shoulder to rest along his cheek, setting his heart reeling. The eyes so near his were almost black, filled with pleading. "Please forgive yourself, Justin. You must know Effie and I lay no blame upon you."

Sincerity filled the sweet, whispered words that began to ease the weight of guilt in his chest. Wonder swept through him that she had come to comfort him.

He gathered her gently closer. His gaze locked with hers and he bent his head, allowing her plenty of time to draw away. Instead, joy flooded him when her soft hand slipped from his cheek to the back of his neck the instant before his lips touched hers.

ten

Justin's kiss was incredibly tender, and Constance ached to stay forever in his arms, her husband's arms.

In the arms of a man who was in love with another woman.

The thought brought her to her senses as effectively as a dunking in ice water. She drew away from his embrace, disappointment swamping her when he released her immediately. What was the matter with her? Hadn't she wanted him to release her? Had she lost all ability to reason, because a man kissed her?

Because the man she loved kissed her. The realization brought a small gasp. She loved him!

Justin caught her lightly by the shoulders. "Have I offended you so? Must I. . .shall I beg your pardon?"

His low words trembled slightly, adding to the turmoil in her chest. She dared not look at him for fear he'd see the love in her eyes. How could she expect him to ask her pardon when she had welcomed his kiss with all of her traitorous heart? Hadn't he realized how her lips had yielded to his?

"There is much I'd like to say to you, Constance, but this isn't the time. It's been a trying evening for both of us. I apologize if I've made it more difficult for you. But I'm grateful for your comfort."

She nodded slightly, noticing his hands clenched at his sides. Was he remembering Marian also, and regretting their embrace? "I. . .thank you for caring so deeply for the children. Good night." She wanted to race for the door and up the steps to her room, but she forced herself to keep a ladylike pace. It wouldn't do to let him know how deeply she'd been affected by the last few minutes.

She glanced in passing at the grandfather clock at the bottom of the stairs. A quarter past midnight, and she was to have met Alex at midnight. The knowledge quickened her steps. In her concern for Justin, she'd forgotten the meeting.

In her room, she pulled her paisley shawl over her white blouse to hide it from the moonlight. Opening her door an inch, she listened tensely for Justin to retire to his room so she could leave the house without risk of being seen. The minutes ticked by with slow regularity, but he did not ascend the stairs.

Her lips still throbbed from his kiss. She wished she could put it from her mind, forget the way it felt to be folded tenderly next to his heart. "I'm grateful for your comfort," he'd said. Likely he had only kissed her in gratitude for her forgiveness over Effie's accident.

Her admiration for him which began on the train had grown as she watched him caring for the children and dealing with the townspeople's contempt. But tonight, after experiencing his pain as though it were her own, she couldn't deny her love for him.

She had never believed love could come so swiftly. But normally one wouldn't have the opportunity to know someone so well within such a short time, her heart argued. One's true character was revealed quickly by life-threatening circumstances such as they'd encountered together.

Love was so much more than her friends had said, more than a delightful fire racing through her veins, as uncontrollable as a magnetic force. It was a sweetness and warmth that filled her at Justin's kindness to her and the children, at his devotion to them and care of them that left her aching with the knowledge it was beyond repayment. She could never be worthy of such a precious love.

Justin had explained to her that according to the Bible marriage is a symbol of the relationship between God and His followers. Now that she'd committed herself to God, she did wish to please Him. The thought of an annulment was unsettling in light of her new faith.

But falling in love with Justin was foolish. It only invited heartbreak. He may have kissed her, but he loved Marian. The knowledge twisted cruelly through her heart.

Well, even if she could never have his love, she could try to give back a portion of the kindness and devotion he gave her and the children, until the case was over and they parted.

"Lord, help me. Show me how to be a blessing to him," she stumbled over the unfamiliar words. "Thank You, whatever the future holds, for these days You've allowed me to spend with him."

Was her prayer sufficient? She was still uncomfortable speaking to God. But Justin had said that would change as time went on, she reminded herself.

A footfall! Finally he was coming up the stairs! She closed her door softly, leaning against it, waiting for his footsteps to pass her room. Had they paused slightly before continuing on? She held her breath until she heard the door to Justin's room open and close.

She hated sneaking out of his house to meet Alex. It was only proper that Justin should know of her position as a Pinkerton operative. She'd tell him tomorrow at the first opportunity, regardless of the Superintendent's command.

The decision lifted some of the weight from her spirit. She latched the back door softly and ran lightly across the lawn to the carriage house. It wouldn't seem so strange if voices were heard there tonight, since Zeke was staying in the second story. The moon was especially bright tonight. She glanced over her shoulder at the softly lit windows of Justin's bedchamber. No sign of him. What would he think if he looked out and saw her? The thought put wings on her feet.

Holding her breath, she carefully lifted the heavy wrought-iron door latch. She'd barely opened the door when a hand clasped her wrist and pulled her inside.

"I thought you'd never get here!"

"Alexander!" The breath she'd caught whooshed out.

"Zeke said Effie wasn't seriously harmed. Has there been a change?"

She shook her head, then realized he couldn't see her in the darkness. "No."

"Knight still acting like a gentleman?"

The memory of his kiss swept back. "Y. . .yes."

"Sounds like you're shivering. Cold?"

"On this warm night? Don't be silly. What news have you for me?"

"I had the minister on the train checked out. Just as Knight said, he's ordained. Nothing to indicate he's tied up with Rasmus Pierce."

This time last night the news would have only added to her frustration. Now, now her heart tied her to Justin more securely than any vows. Married or not, she loved him.

"How is Knight getting along without the money he lost in the robbery?"

Shock burst through her like a lightning bolt. She tried to speak, but her vocal chords were paralyzed.

"Did you hear me?"

Her fingers pressed against her throat. "I didn't know Justin had any money in the express car. I assume you are speaking of the train robbery?"

"Right. A good piece of the money belonged to him, almost $50,000."

Constance flattened her hands against the wall behind her. She wished she could see something to sit upon. Her knees were threatening to fail her.

"There must be some mistake."

"It's no mistake. The Superintendent believes Knight was in on the robbery."

"Surely you are jesting!"

"Not a bit of it. Superintendent is usually right about these things. If he's correct this time, your position in Knight's home, much as I hate it, is a gift. Has he said anything that might substantiate his guilt?"

She tried unsuccessfully to push aside the pain tearing through her. As Alex said, the Superintendent was seldom wrong about these matters. Experience on other cases had taught her that a woman's heart wasn't a good judge of a man's character. But this time, it was *her* heart!

Reluctantly, she scanned her memory, terrified of finding incriminating evidence. All of Justin's actions appeared honorable. Relief unknotted the tension in her stomach.

"I can think of nothing to condemn him."

"Start keeping a watch out with the possibility Knight is in this with Pierce. If you get a chance, go through his papers." He snorted. "Why am I telling you what to do? You're one of Pinkerton's best operatives. You know what to do."

The knot was back in her stomach, tighter than ever.

"Yes. I know what to do. I'd best get back. If Effie calls for me, Justin will discover I'm out." Besides, there was a very good chance the tears burning her eyelids were about to let loose in a shower, and she didn't want Alex around if that happened. There was nothing more foolish than falling in love with a suspect!

Moonlight streamed in the door when Alex pushed it open, silent on its new hinges.

"Be careful, Constance. Knight's life isn't worth yours."

She nodded, no longer trusting her voice.

The night air felt good against her hot cheeks as she hurried back to the house. She wished it could blow away the horrible suspicion Alex had planted.

She wouldn't be telling Justin she was an operative after all. She'd been feeling guilty for deceiving him. Was he deceiving her instead? Had he and Rasmus somehow discovered on the train that she was an operative? Did they think that by marrying her to Justin they could remove her from actively pursuing Rasmus and remove any suspicion of Justin's involvement with Rasmus at the same time?

When she finally slipped between the lavender-scented sheets in the room meant for Marian, she buried her face in her pillow to keep her sobs from passing through the wall to Justin's bedchamber. It had been difficult enough realizing she'd fallen in love with him knowing he was in love with Marian. But to think he might be so dishonorable as to be a thief! It was more than she could bear.

eleven

With Justin spending his days at the bank, Constance had ample time to search his room and library. She did so with dread. Would she unearth something that would tumble Justin from the lofty position in which her heart held him?

She found no money, notes, or bonds in the house. Nor did she see any sign of a safe or other likely hiding place.

In his library desk drawer, she found a carved box filled with bills for the house and furnishings. The number of them took her breath. Had these bills driven him to a desperate act?

If it weren't for the suspicion planted by Alexander, she would have rather enjoyed life with Justin. During the days she supervised the servants, shopped, or visited Libby. In the evenings, he took time to play with the children and have a family time of Bible reading and prayers. The children had begun attending the first grade level of school, and were full of tales each evening.

After the children were in bed, he would work at his desk. Constance joined him in the library, doing needlework or reading. Often she spent the time reading the Bible. Justin was never too busy to set aside his work and answer the questions that invariably arose during her readings.

Occasionally she'd glance up to find his gaze on her with an expression that sent her heart pattering wildly, though he hadn't attempted to kiss her again or broach an intimate conversation.

The role of Mrs. Justin Knight was the most difficult she'd ever attempted. Over the years she'd played a gypsy, a wealthy socialite, a nurse, a young widow, and a poor type writer, among other things. As Mrs. Justin Knight, she played herself. Except she couldn't reveal her vocation, or tell her husband she loved him. And she might be working to put the man she loved in prison. Her heart clutched at the thought. How could anything so difficult be asked of one?

If only he would mention the loss of his money in the robbery, she thought. *Why didn't he tell me of it? Why?*

Constance spent as much time as she could spare visiting with Libby. The woman was always full of town gossip. It helped keep Constance's mind off Justin and the constant fear that the Superintendent's suspicions might prove true. There was also the possibility that something her aunt innocently revealed in her tattles would provide a hint that would lead to apprehending Rasmus.

One day she tried to casually introduce a topic often in her mind since her last talk with Alex.

"Have you heard any rumors about Mr. Knight's bank? Being a businesswoman, I thought perhaps you would hear things I would not. You know how tight-lipped husband's are about business."

Libby's busy hands stopped tugging at the black lace and silk flowers adorning a straw hat. Her steel-gray eyebrows lifted in surprise.

"Now, dearie, what would make you suspect your husband of having business troubles?"

Constance settled a broad-brimmed leghorn on her black hair and looked into the viewing mirror, trying to appear casual.

"The last few years haven't been healthy for banks. And then, Mr. Ames did threaten that people would remove their funds from Justin's bank."

"I haven't heard of any run on his bank. Marian's father was just letting out some temper."

"There's the new house, too. It must have cost Justin something dear."

"Mr. Knight deals with money every day. I doubt he'd over-extend himself." Her long, thin fingers closed about the brim of the leghorn. "Here, dear, allow me to adjust this for you." Deftly she folded up the back brim and attached it to the crown with a glittering black jet butterfly. "There! Isn't that better?"

"Yes," Constance replied absently. "Then you haven't heard of workmen complaining of overdue bills for the house?"

Fists propped on her navy skirt, Libby set her narrow lips in a prim line. "Workmen wouldn't know what to do with their lips if they weren't complaining of overdue bills. Now, I expect you'll place your trust in Mr. Knight and not ask any further indelicate questions."

How was a woman to place trust in her husband when a Pinkerton superintendent was suggesting that same husband might be involved in unsavory crimes?

She longed to confide in Libby. It would be nice to have someone help her sort out her thoughts and feelings. But what could she tell her? It was unthinkable to share information regarding a case.

And concerning Justin, what could she say? "The most awful thing has happened. I've fallen in love with my husband."

She groaned. Her aunt would think her feebleminded.

☙

That evening when the family gathered in the parlor for devotions, Justin stopped Effie beneath a softly-shaded lamp and propped her round chin up with his fingers.

"It's been over a week since your accident. How is your face feeling?"

"Good."

It was an awfully colorful face, Constance thought. The swelling had gone down a bit, but her nose and eyes were the colors of the room: blue, yellow, and magenta.

Justin chose the fourteenth chapter of John for the text that evening. One verse stood out especially clear in Constance's mind: Jesus saying, "I am the way, the truth and the life. No man cometh unto the Father, but by me."

The way, the *truth,* and the life. Her thoughts stuck on the phrase, and she didn't hear the rest of Justin's reading. She felt as though the word "deceiver" were blazoned in large letters across her forehead.

What would Jesus, who was *the truth,* think of her profession? She'd always thought of her vocation as promoting justice and banishing evil. But what would Christ think of using deception for such an end? There was so much she had to learn of Him!

"Shall we pray?" Justin's question brought her back to the present in time to see Evan and Effie, seated on either side of her, folding their hands and bowing their heads. Effie's long shiny brown curls slid forward and hid her cheeks. Evan's legs stuck straight beyond the end of the cushion, the blues in his favorite sailor suit almost black against the china blue damask.

She always listened closely to Justin's prayers, trying to learn the proper manner to speak to God, in spite of his insistence that there wasn't such a thing, only a proper attitude of heart and mind.

"Dear Lord and Father," Justin began in his rich voice, "I thank Thee for the pleasure Thou hast given me by bringing each of the people in this room into my life. Please make me the man Thou wouldst have me to be for Effie and Evan. Teach me how to be a help to Constance during this trying time. Thank Thee for her infinite patience, and the peace and order she brings to our home. In Christ's name, Amen."

Tears stung behind Constance's eyelids. *Did he mean those words?* She daren't meet his gaze, for fear he'd see in her eyes the love for him that was growing daily.

"What'th a 'trying time'?" Effie was leaning forward, hands still clasped in her lap, brows meeting in puzzlement.

"It's when things aren't the way we wish."

"But thith ithn't a trying time," she protested. "We like

being married to you."

"Yes," Evan agreed promptly. "We like the big house and the Bird Cage, and the pony and cart. And you, too, Justin."

A smile broke across Constance's face at the last comment, and destroyed her resolve to keep her gaze away from Justin.

"Glad to hear it, old man."

"Maybe Aunt Conthtanth wouldn't think it a trying time if you gave her a pony and cart."

"Effie!" Laughter tangled with disapproval in Constance's exclamation.

"I guess that's something to consider. Thank you for the advice." His amused glance met Constance's.

He could be such fun! If only they weren't caught in this untenable situation. Perhaps under normal circumstances, he would have fallen in love with her, and there would be a chance for a real future together for them.

Except that under "normal circumstances," Marian would be Justin's wife now. The thought drove the joy from her heart and brought her to her feet. She held her hands out to the twins.

"Time to dress for bed, dears."

Effie rested a pudgy hand on Justin's knee. "Will you come up to kith uth goodnight?"

"I will. I couldn't sleep without your hugs."

It would be difficult for the children when the time came to leave him, Constance thought as they went up the stairway together.

It would be difficult for her, too, but at least she knew what to expect, could try to protect herself against future pain, though the longer they stayed here, the more it seemed her attempts were like too few sandbags piled against a rapidly rising river.

Half-an-hour later Justin pulled the door to the Bird Cage closed.

After the way his prayer had touched her heart, Constance didn't dare spend the rest of the evening across the library from him in the usual manner.

"Good night." She hoped her bright smile would keep from him any suspicion of her tangled emotional state. At his surprised look, she added, "I must take care of some correspondence. There are so many people to keep in touch with when one is away from home."

"Please join me first. There's something I must say to you."

A tension underscored his words, sending shivers of apprehension along her nerves. As much as she wanted to give herself a chance to repair her barriers against her attraction to him, she couldn't deny his request.

In the library, he stepped behind the desk. Constance stood on the opposite side, linked her fingers together in front of her skirt, and watched him silently. His mouth was a tight line in his rigid face. What had he to tell her? She breathed slowly, trying to calm the mad thudding of her heart.

He clasped his hands behind him. "A widow, Mrs. Healy, was in the bank today. Her husband was once one of the wealthiest men in town. In the recent difficult financial times, he turned most of his investments into cash with which to keep his company afloat. In addition, he borrowed heavily. With the common belief that a gentleman doesn't burden a woman with business problems, Mr. Healy kept the facts from his wife. When he died last month, Mrs. Healy was shocked to discover she is no longer a wealthy woman, but barely a step beyond poverty."

What had this story to do with her?, Constance thought. The eyes that met hers were black with repressed emotion. A deep breath lifted his jacket, and he squared his shoulders. Opening a drawer, he pulled forth the carved box which she knew to be filled with slips of debt for this house.

Opening the cover, he let it rest against its hinges and pulled out a handful of bills. He tossed them to the desktop, where they spilled out in a fanlike pattern. "My debts." His voice was tight. "For this house and furnishings. I had thought they would be paid in full by now. Rasmus' robbery of the express car changed that."

"Why are you telling me this now?"

"Mrs. Healy's situation made me aware of how selfish and proud it is for a man to keep all knowledge of a couple's affairs to himself."

"But. . ."

He held up a broad palm. "I know you do not consider us truly married." Bitterness iced his words. "I'm not going to argue the facts with you at present. If something happens to me, if I die before Rasmus is apprehended, the law will consider us married, and my debts will become yours. You have a right to know that."

If he died! A shiver rolled over her.

His face twisted violently. "I'm sorry."

She longed to tell him that it wasn't the thought of debt that had scared her, but she couldn't admit how dear he'd become to her.

"I don't wonder you stand there staring at me in horror, Constance. It seems Rasmus' attempt to keep Marian from me never ceases to complicate your life."

She lowered herself onto a nearby leather chair, her hands grasping the wide walnut arms.

"You deal with money daily. How did you arrive at such a state as this?"

He snorted and dropped into the tall leather swivel chair, resting his elbows on the desk. His hands plowed through his hair.

"I was concentrating too much on bank business and not enough on my personal finances. I'd given Marian a free hand in furbishing the house, though I stated the limitations on funds I'd planned for the project. She spent far more than I allowed. I'm not excusing myself. I should have asked for a regular accounting. But I spent the time and effort on bank business instead."

"Why did you indicate that the express car theft hampered your ability to meet your debts?"

"I'd been to Chicago to sell property that I'd inherited on Prairie Avenue."

"But that's one of the wealthiest sections of the city. Real estate prices there are very high."

"The prices I received for the sales would have almost paid off these debts. Now Rasmus will be spending the money instead."

She rose, her eyes meeting his steadily.

"Thank you for sharing your financial situation with me. I hope you will find a solution. Alexander said there's no sign of unexpectedly large purchases made in the area recently. Perhaps the thieves won't have spent the money before it's recovered."

"Rasmus has been at large for a good while. I admit to having reservations about the Pinkertons' ability to apprehend him."

"The agency has a commendable reputation."

"That they do," he admitted grudgingly. "Whatever happens, I hope you'll not become responsible for my debts."

"That hasn't happened yet." She crossed to the door and paused, her hand on the woodwork, to seek his dear face across the room. "And if it should happen, you would be forgiven."

She strode quickly from the room, not wanting him to see the truth in her eyes, that she would forgive him almost anything. But she hadn't turned quickly enough to miss the widening of his own eyes, warmly brown in the soft light from the desk lamp.

❧

Justin's gaze met hers across the dimly lit room. Her voice was like the richest velvet: "If it should happen, you would be forgiven."

Justin's heart stopped, then plunged on thunderously. *Could she possibly mean the promise in her words and voice?*

"Constance!"

He stepped toward her, but she whirled about and disappeared into the hallway like a frightened doe.

For a moment he was tempted to follow her, take her in his arms and not let her go until she admitted the love she'd hinted at. Common sense stopped him. It was too soon. If love for him was beginning to flicker in her heart, he didn't want to extinguish it by rushing her. He'd promised when she moved into his home not to make demands on her; he meant to keep his word.

It had been extremely difficult honoring that promise during the week that had passed since Effie's accident, the night he'd taken Constance in his arms and kissed her. His arms had felt empty ever since. Her lips had yielded to his so sweetly, and so briefly. But she hadn't demanded the apology he'd offered, and the knowledge left his heart brimming with hope.

His mouth spread in a smile. *Lord willing, I'll win her love yet.*

❧

"Constance!"

She ignored his soft, eager call and hurried up the wide, sweeping stairway. She had endured all she could of his sweet presence tonight.

She continued all the way to the Bird Cage on the third floor, where she checked on the children. They were sound asleep, Effie's arms thrown back in abandonment, Evan's tucked beneath his pillow. They were such dears! When this case was over and the marriage issue resolved, would she be able to leave them with Libby and return to her work in Chicago as originally intended? It would be like tearing out part of her heart. She hadn't realized when the plans were made how much a part of her life they had become.

The breeze through the open portals was cool against her

cheeks, fragrant with the spicy scent of geraniums from the boxes attached to the railings.

Justin had finally told her of his money stolen from the express car. She had been waiting and hoping for this since Alex's revelation days ago. Why then did it give her no joy? Why was her chest taut with pain and fear? Did Justin's sharing not indicate his trust in her? Did it not indicate he wasn't party to Rasmus Pierce's crimes?

Or did it mean he knew she was a Pinkerton operative? Had he somehow discovered that Alex had told her of Justin's loss, and told her of it himself only to avert suspicion?

"No, it's not possible." She could barely hear her own whisper. "Justin is a Christian. He would never conspire with Rasmus."

Wouldn't he? How could she be certain? What did she actually know about him? Except that he held her heart.

She stared unseeingly at a row of distant street lamps in the business section near the always-active riverfront. There had been the well-known Pinkerton case involving Michael Rogers. Mr. Rogers was a wealthy man, a "pillar" of the Methodist Church in Council Bluffs, Iowa. Local authorities had laughed at Mr. Pinkerton when he told them of his suspicions. Yet it was eventually proven that Mr. Rogers was a member of the infamous Reno gang.

But there was more to being a Christian than being an upstanding churchman. Thanks to Justin, she knew now that it was Christ in one's life that made one a Christian. Justin carried his faith into every aspect of his life.

At least, into every aspect he allowed her to see. Such a disquieting thought.

The breeze was suddenly cold. She wrapped her arms over her chest, rubbing her palms briskly over her upper arms, crushing her voluminous, pleated white sleeves in the process.

Moonbeams danced over the children's round faces. She

stopped to tuck the blankets about them more securely. They looked so angelic in sleep! How they loved Justin. She hated to think of the pain it was going to cause them to leave him.

She understood Libby's comment about Rasmus' mother now. If Justin was a criminal, she couldn't condemn him or be ashamed of him. She would only hurt, achingly, eternally hurt, for the choices he made that kept happiness from his life.

Tears pricked at her eyelids, and her heart echoed the unspoken cry in her mind, "Lord, don't let Justin be guilty!"

twelve

Constance stood outside Aunt Libby's shop, Evan and Effie on either side of her, waiting for the clanging red and gold trolley to pass. The moment it was safe, the children darted across the street, adeptly dodging pedestrians and horsedrawn vehicles.

She shook her head resignedly as she followed. The stop at Pierce's General Store following the almost daily visit to Libby's millinery was becoming an eagerly-awaited ritual.

She paused for a wagon to pass, smiling at the driver when she recognized Mr. Meeker. He lifted his broad brimmed, sweat-stained brown hat and nodded to her cheerfully. He'd been at the store a few times when she stopped, usually delivering crops or baked goods in exchange for supplies, and Mrs. Pierce had introduced them. The last time she saw him, he'd mentioned that his bride of a year had returned to Missouri for a few weeks to see her ailing mother. She wondered idly when she'd return.

Her brow wrinkled in a frown as she hurried toward the store. Libby continued to insist her wardrobe inadequate for the wife of such a grand man as Justin. Constance did not intend to add to his pile of debts, and she certainly would not share the news of his financial problems with Aunt Libby, even if she had shared it with Alexander. She'd hated the gleam of satisfaction her news brought to her fellow operative's eyes.

Her concentration was so complete, she almost collided with a tall man in a gray suit. She stepped back quickly, the man's hands steadying her.

"Justin!" Joy at the unexpected encounter danced like sun-beams on her heart.

He smiled down at her. "Where to in such a hurry?"

"Following the children to the general store. They love to stop at the candy display there."

"I should think they would prefer the wider selection at the confectionery. Under the circumstances, I'm surprised you choose to shop at Pierce's."

She ignored his guardedly curious look.

"The children must always part with their precious pennies at the confectionery, but Mrs. Pierce has been known to *give* them each a piece of candy on occasion."

"Not tough-as-flint Mrs. Pierce? When I was a boy, she chased me and my friends from the store with her broom more times than I could count."

"Due to your fine manners, no doubt."

His twinkling eyes sent her heart tripping. "But what else? It was during our Robin Hood period."

She stopped short. "Robin Hood? You don't mean. . ."

A melodramatic sigh accompanied his nod. "Afraid so. We thought it chivalrous to take her candy sticks and give them to the poor new immigrant kids."

"It never occurred to you to purchase the candy?"

"That was impossible. Robin never paid for the food he gave away, you see."

Dismay spread across her chest. Did he have a natural criminal tendency, or had he merely been a typical lad?

"Of course, when our parents discovered what we'd been doing, we had to pay every cent back, by the sweat of our brows."

"I would consider it a personal favor if you kept the exploits of your wayward youth from Effie and Evan."

His chuckle won her smile as they entered the store.

She spotted Evan and Effie at the candy counter, as usual, near a young blonde woman speaking with Mrs. Pierce.

Her attention on the children, she barely noticed the cheap glasses and kerosene lamps she passed that lined the window shelves, sparkling in the sunlight. The prisms of a hanging gas lamp sent miniature rainbows darting about the aisle and merchandise, but her attention was on the woman beside Effie. Could it be Marian?

Mrs. Pierce smiled. "Good day, Mrs. Knight."

The blonde's shoulders stiffened beneath gold braid on violet silk, but she didn't turn about.

"Hello. I hope Effie and Evan haven't been any trouble." The children paid no attention to her arrival, but continued a whispered argument over which candies to purchase.

"Those two dears? I should say not. Brightens my day to have them stop." Constance watched the pale eyes in the age-lined, skinny face move over her shoulder to where Justin stood. "We don't often have the pleasure of your company, Mr. Knight."

The blonde's gloved fingers tightened on the glass countertop. Constance was certain now that it was Marian.

"Mrs. Kelly usually does my shopping for me."

Marian swung around to face them, blue eyes sparking above her perfect, tiny nose. Despair swept through Constance. How could she ever hope that Justin might fall in love with her? Marian had captured his heart, and she was as different from petite, fair-haired, fiery-spirited Marian as River's Edge from Chicago.

The young woman's pointed chin lifted. "It seems *some* woman is always doing your shopping for you, Mr. Knight."

The pile of bills Marian had charged flashed on Constance's mind.

Before Justin could respond to Marian's challenge, she continued. "I don't believe I've had the pleasure of being introduced to your wife."

Constance allowed him to pull her hand through his arm and keep it firmly in place with his clasp. "Mrs. Knight, this is Miss Marian Ames. Miss Ames, my wife."

Constance inclined her head slightly. "It's a pleasure to meet you, Miss Ames."

Marian's eyes were hard as sapphires. "Thank you."

Justin ignored her rude reply. "And these are Mrs. Knight's niece and nephew, Effie and Evan Ward, who live with us."

At their names, the children turned. Noticing Justin holding his derby, Evan whipped off his round straw hat. Justin gave him a solemn wink of approval.

Marian barely glanced at the children. Her attention was fully on Justin. "I shouldn't keep you. I only stopped to speak with my future mother-in-law."

"You're to be married?"

The shock in Justin's voice was reflected by the muscle which jumped in the arm beneath Constance's hand.

"Yes. To Rasmus."

Justin's face was whiter than death. Pain shot through Constance at the way his eyes grew old before her. Was he thinking he had lost Marian's love forever? That he couldn't bear it?

Marian's face glowed with satisfaction at her announcement's effect, and anger rippled through Constance. *Wasn't it enough that she hurt Justin horribly? Must she gloat over it?*

"Ith Rathmuth the man from the train?"

Constance nodded. "Yes, Effie."

Effie's red cotton gown swung as she whirled to face Marian. "You muthn't marry him. Rathmuth ith a mean man. He pointed a gun at Evan on the train and made Aunt Conthtanth marry Juthtin."

"Effie!"

"Effie!"

Constance's protest was effectually lost in Justin's roar, which brought dusky color back to his face.

"Is it true?"

Pity flooded Constance at Marian's husky whisper.

Evan grabbed his sister's arm and shook it. "We weren't s'posed to tell!"

Effie dug her few remaining top teeth into her bottom lip,

and looked cautiously at Constance. "I forgot."

"It is true." Marian's sounded desperate. "If it weren't, the children wouldn't have been ordered not to speak of it." A sob burst from her. She pushed her way past them to tear down the narrow aisle.

"Marian!"

Constance clutched at Justin's arm as he started after her. "We must help Mrs. Pierce!"

The woman was leaning weakly against the countertop, her face as gray as her work gown.

Justin reached her before Constance did. With strong hands below her shoulders, he lowered her to the rickety chair behind the counter before she slumped.

"Fainted. See if you can find some spirits of ammonia."

She searched quickly among the crowded counters and returned with the bottle. Justin had loosened the high collar of Mrs. Pierce's gown and untied the long apron which covered it.

It was only moments before Mrs. Pierce revived, though her eyes looked so tragic that Constance wondered if it wouldn't have been a kindness to allow her to remain oblivious to the world a few minutes longer.

The woman struggled weakly to sit up by herself, but Justin kept a hand below her arm.

"Take it easy, Mrs. Pierce. You've no other customers at present. Rest a few minutes."

"Rest." The tired voice cracked on the word. Wrinkled lids covered the washed-out blue eyes. "Do you think the mother of Rasmus Pierce can ever rest? I tell myself there isn't anythin' new in crime or plain deviltry that he can do. But always he finds more ways to hurt people." The lids opened slowly. Her troubled gaze rested on Justin's face. "I'm sorry he wrecked your plans to marry Miss Ames. I didn't know."

He smiled through tight lips. "It doesn't matter. The woman I married instead is superb, don't you agree?"

Constance's heart felt as though it would burst. *If only he meant it!*

Wrinkled fingers plucked at his sleeve. "But Miss Ames, she's young and headstrong. No tellin' what Rasmus will do if she accuses him of ruinin' her marriage to you."

"I'll try to locate her and explain everything. But not until I know you're well."

She straightened bony shoulders beneath the thin cambric dress.

"I've lived through a lot of things in my time, boy. Expect I'll make it through this, too." Her skinny, blue-veined hand patted one of his. "I'd give my life to have had my boy turn out as fine as you."

Even Effie and Evan were still subdued when the four left the store upon the arrival of Mr. Pierce a few minutes later.

Settling beside Constance on the wide, red leather seat beneath the black fringed carriage top, Justin picked up the reins.

"I have to try locate her."

Constance nodded. Of course he meant Marian.

"If she says anything to Rasmus, and if I know Marian she'll repeat what she's heard loudly and completely, it could mean trouble. He won't like it that she's found out."

"I know." She kept her voice low, like his. It wouldn't do to frighten the children who were in the seat behind them. *Was he remembering*, as she was, *the wedding gift?* Remembering how easy it was for Rasmus to enter their home? Could they protect the children should Rasmus decide to carry out his threat?

"I'll leave you and the children at the house. Zeke will be there with you. I'll tell him what's happened before I leave."

She nodded. Zeke's presence would help, of course. But she felt safer with Justin close, in spite of the Superintendent's suspicions. She laid her hand in its soft black glove on his arm. She kept her eyes on it even when she knew he was looking down at her in surprise.

"Please, hurry back to us, Justin."

❧

But when the twilight faded into night and the lights warmed the house against the darkness, he still hadn't returned.

Constance alternately stared out draped windows watching for him, and paced the floor until she was sure the new, thick carpet would be in tatters by morning.

Zeke had gone up to bed with the children. His plan was to sleep on the floor inside their door. They'd led the children to believe his presence was a special treat for them. The twins had been allowed to bring cookies and milk to their room, and Zeke had promised to tell them stories.

"Keep them safe, Lord, please." She repeated her plea for the fiftieth time since Justin left. She'd felt so sure of the Pinkertons' ability to protect people in the past, but this time it was Effie and Evan being guarded, and the famous company's reputation didn't reassure her one whit.

A lantern glowed outside the carriage house, then went out.

That would be Alexander's signal. She hurried through the kitchen and out the back door. Wind snatched it from her hands to slam it against the wall. She struggled to shut it.

The wind pulled at her hair and green skirt as she bent against it. The derringer she'd slipped into the embroidered muslin pocket hanging beneath her skirt was heavy against her hip. She didn't intend to be caught without it again should Rasmus appear.

A hand on her arm sent her heart hurtling to the ground and back. The grip kept her from reaching her derringer. *Rasmus?*

"Constance, it's Alex."

Relief almost took the stiffening from her knees. "Thank the Lord it is you!"

His voice was at her ear. "Can't hear you with this wind. Guess you couldn't hear me, either. I called to you twice." He pulled open the door and they slipped inside.

The friendly smell of leather from new harnesses hanging

on the wall greeted them. At the sound of a small scratch, sulfur filled the air and a long match flickered.

"Did you hear what happened at Pierce's Store?" Constance asked breathlessly.

His dark eyes peered at her through the small blue and yellow flame. "No."

Quickly she poured out the story, reminding him of Rasmus' threat to harm the children if Marian discovered the truth about Justin's and Constance's marriage. Long before she'd finished, Alex had shaken out the match.

"Zeke went looking for you as soon as Justin left this afternoon, Alex. He couldn't stay away long. We were both concerned for the children."

"Of course. Their protection must come first, at all costs."

She breathed a sigh of relief. She hadn't been certain he would feel that way.

"We'll need to have an agent watch Marian. Obviously she's been in contact with Rasmus. We should have thought of that angle earlier."

Yes, they should have. *What would Rasmus do when Marian spoke to him? Would he harm her?* The thought sent shivers up Marion's arms.

"I'd best get started. Sooner we begin watching the Ames' home the better."

A minute later he was closing the carriage house door behind them, and they were back in the wind.

He started to say something and she leaned nearer to hear him, bending her head until it almost touched his shoulder. His hand was at her waist, steadying her against the buffeting winds.

"Be careful, Constance. Keep your derringer at hand. We're up against a bad one this time."

She lifted her head to reply, but she never had the chance. He was torn from beside her and thrown against the door.

She grasped for the pocket with the derringer.

"Keep your hands off my wife, Bixby!"

Even the wind couldn't hide Justin's yell. It stilled her reach for the gun and sent her heart plummeting. When had he come? They hadn't heard his horse's hoofs.

Alex pushed himself to a standing position, straightened his coat, stepped closer to make himself heard, though he, too, had to yell to accomplish it.

"You've got it wrong, Knight. We're talking about the case."

"Why not meet at the house if that's true? Get out of here, and quick."

Constance clutched at Justin's lapels. "Don't be foolish. We need him. We can't protect the children or apprehend Rasmus without him."

Bixby flexed the shoulder that had hit the side of the house with force at Justin's earlier shove. "We're all in this together, Knight. We may not like each other, but we can at least be civil."

"Just keep your hands off my wife, understand? Now get off my property."

Alex leaned down and picked up the hat that had flown to the ground at Justin's attack, crushed it on his wind-blown hair, nodded at Constance, and shouted, "Remember what I said!"

Justin's grip remained on Constance's arm until they entered the kitchen, where he released her abruptly.

She shoved back the wisps of hair the wind had pulled from their pins and tossed across her face. "What enticed you to act so abominably? Alexander is helping us."

"Helping himself to my wife." The words snapped with anger. "He told me he's in love with you, expects to marry you when Rasmus is behind bars."

"But I. . ."

"You may as well get him out of your mind and heart. You're married to me, and you'll stay so."

thirteen

"You're married to me and you'll stay so!"

Those angry words had been going around in Constance's mind like a steamboat wheel. *Won't they ever stop?*

Constance slipped the purple bolero vest trimmed with black braid over her white shirtwaist. Tugging slightly at the bottom of the vest to straighten it, she looked in the floor-length swinging mirror. The vest went perfectly with her new purple and ivory striped skirt.

Round amethysts surrounded by tiny seed pearls dangled daintily in gold from her ears. It was nice to wear something other than silver and onyx mourning jewelry.

"Hoping to cheer yourself with the earrings and your new outfit, aren't you?" she asked her reflection. "Neither has removed the bags from beneath your eyes."

No wonder. She hadn't slept a wink all night. Justin's accusing eyes and voice had kept her company no matter how hard she'd tried to push them away. It hurt unbearably to think he believed she'd meet Alexander clandestinely. If she could tell him she was an agent. . . .

That still wasn't an option.

She'd best be starting downstairs. Mrs. Kelly would likely have breakfast prepared soon.

The enticing odors of coffee and sausage greeted her when she entered the hallway. She poked her head into the children's room and urged them to hurry their dressing. She'd learned months ago that they no longer appreciated her offers to help.

She hesitated halfway down the stairs. Justin was leaning against the library door reading a newspaper. Her heart lurched when he looked up and saw her. She continued her descent, resisting the desire to turn and bolt back up the stairs.

He folded the newspaper briskly and tucked it beneath one arm. Stepping forward, he waited for her at the bottom of the stairway. The eyes that had always been so warm and friendly were shuttered. The determined line of his mouth set her trembling inside. The man obviously had something to say and intended to say it.

Didn't he say enough last night? At the memory, heat filled her face. She stopped on the last step, hand resting on the smooth balustrade.

"Good morning."

"Good morning. I wanted to speak with you first thing."

That was obvious. "Have you more indiscretions of which to accuse me?"

He winced at her comment, and she hated herself immediately for having made it. She might hear what he had to say before attacking him. If the gray shadows beneath his eyes were any indication, he hadn't slept well last night, either.

"I thought you should know that I wasn't able to locate Marian yesterday."

His formal, reserved tone assured her she wasn't yet forgiven for last night and sparked her anger.

"When you didn't return until so late, I was sure you'd found her and the two of you were having a heart-to-heart conversation." Or that Rasmus had found them together and harmed him, but she wasn't about to let him know she'd feared for his safety. Her heart was too raw from last night's vocal beating.

Even his lips grew white at her taunt. "I haven't spoken to Marian out of your presence since we married."

How easily that term slipped off his tongue—"since we married." The words always had to struggle through her throat.

"Constance, we need to put aside our differences and think of the children. If Marian has reached Rasmus, we cannot guard Effie and Evan too closely."

He was right, of course. She shifted her eyes from his tense face. She couldn't indulge her pain at the expense of the children.

"Zeke slept in their room last night."

"No he didn't. I did."

"You. . .!"

"I stopped to check on them before retiring. Zeke almost knocked me out before we recognized each other. I sent him back to the carriage house, and I took his place. I thought it would look pretty strange if anyone discovered he'd spent the night in our house instead of his room."

"Of course." How would they have explained such a thing to Mrs. Kelly? She hadn't even thought of it when she and Zeke concocted the plan. But then, the children's safety had been uppermost in their minds.

"Now that we've come to a cease fire. . . ."

Her hands clutched the banister and she took a shaky breath. "Before the subject is entirely put to rest, there's something I'd like to say."

His gaze locked with hers. "I'm waiting."

"In spite of the fact that I entered into this marriage with the expectation it would be temporary, I would not be unfaithful to our vows while the marriage exists. I did not meet Alexander for indiscreet or unsavory purposes. I met him to tell him of Marian's engagement to Rasmus."

"Why should he care what Marian does?"

She struggled to beat down the anger flamed by his contempt. "If she's meeting Rasmus, the Pinkerton agents can follow her to locate him. At least, that's what Alexander said they would do when I spoke with him."

His gaze bored into her eyes, searching their depths as if to discover the truth. She met his scrutiny unflinchingly.

He wasn't the only one with doubts. Her heart still tried to override her reason and say Justin was innocent of connection with Rasmus. But was he? What if her heart was wrong?

What if she told him she was a Pinkerton agent, only to discover he *was* a partner with Rasmus? In such a case, he might decide to get rid of her, and then what would happen to the children?

A pounding at the double doors a few feet away broke the strained silence. A glance through the etched glass revealed a round, middle-aged man with a red handlebar mustache and a derby that appeared two sizes too small.

"Sheriff Tucker! What in the world can he want?" Justin had the door open almost before the words were out of his mouth. "Come in, Tucker. What's the news?"

Constance's breath caught in her throat. *The sheriff! Could he have news of Rasmus?* Had the local authorities captured him?

The rotund man took time to tip his derby to Constance. His face was florid. "Excuse me for intruding."

"Please give it no thought. We know you wouldn't do so without cause."

"Cause! I'll say I have cause!" he managed between puffs. "It's your bank, Mr. Knight. It's been robbed!"

❧

There was no doubt in anyone's mind that Rasmus and his gang had performed the heist.

Dynamite had been used to explode the door to the vault. In the noise of the storm, the explosion went undetected until the chief clerk opened the bank for the workday. Debris was scattered throughout the building from the force of the explosion. Numerous repairs were required.

Three evenings later, Constance sat in the wing chair across the room from Justin's desk, the Bible open in her lap.

Justin worked in his shirtsleeves, striped in wine and white tonight. He rested his forehead on his fist and studied the financial statements before him. His hair was in disarray from running his fingers through it. Her heart twisted at the sight of his face, gray with exhaustion, carved with lines that hadn't been there when they met on the train.

Depositors had barely given him a moment's peace for worrying over their lost savings. She sympathized with them, but Justin felt personally responsible for each loss, and she feared the burden was too great for him.

To make matters worse, Marian Ames had disappeared. No one had seen her since the robbery was discovered. Her parents were frantic. Was Justin's heart just as frantic over her safety?

Justin was certain Marian had contacted Rasmus and Constance expected he was correct. One more matter for which he felt responsible. When he'd heard of her disappearance, barely repressed fury had burned in his eyes.

"Deception! It never breeds anything but trouble."

She bit back the sigh that threatened and moved to his desk. "Won't you retire? It's nearly midnight."

He rubbed his hands over his face. "Not yet."

Rising, he straightened his shoulders and moved out from behind the desk, holding out his hand to her. "Will you sit with me?"

She hesitated only a moment before placing her hand in his. It was the first time he had touched her since finding her with Alexander, and she quivered inside. Her heart ached for the camaraderie they'd so briefly shared.

They sat side by side on the sofa. His gaze was locked on their hands, where he played idly with her fingers.

"Did I tell you that the night the bank was robbed, we were holding $70,000 in payroll for one of the local lumber mills?"

"It was in the newspaper."

"$70,000. All those workers without wages. I've arranged with some of the local merchants to give credit to the employees until they receive their next pay, but that will be weeks away."

That was so like him. Admiration surged through her.

"Insurance will only cover a portion of the loss. If Rasmus

isn't apprehended, I don't know how I shall make restitution to the lumber mill, to say nothing of the other depositors. I may need to sell this house. It won't be a great help, since the sale would barely cover the unpaid cost of building and furnishing the home. The law doesn't require me to make restitution, but I can't live in a fine home like this while the lumber mill employees go without money they've worked hard to obtain."

"Of course not." Tears glistened on her lashes, blurring his profile.

"The owner of the mill is worried about the forest fires raging in Wisconsin and northern Minnesota, too. They've been burning for two weeks, and destroyed not only thousands of acres of trees, but a few small towns. The mill owner may have to let some of his men go if his lumber supply is affected. Which means the men need that payroll more than ever."

The strain in his dear face was like an enemy. If only she had a solution to offer, some comfort to give, Constance thought. But she could only think of platitudes that would appear patronizing and be of no true benefit.

"I've no major investments left to liquidate since selling the Prairie Avenue property in Chicago. Of course, Rasmus has his dirty paws on that money, also."

He swallowed hard. "I've decided to make Rasmus an offer. He can keep the portion of the train and bank money that belongs to me if he will return the rest. In exchange, neither the railroad, express company, nor bank will press charges."

Such compromises were common, she knew. Usually they were arranged through secret negotiations by a lawyer retained by the thieves. Pinkerton had always detested such compromises. He felt it imperative that robbers not be allowed to negotiate as though they were law-abiding businessmen. She had always agreed.

"Are you certain this is the only way?"

"Yes." The word was sharp and harsh.

"How do you propose to contact Rasmus?"

"Through an ad in the local newspaper."

In spite of Justin's pain, a ray of joy touched her heart. She was finally convinced beyond a doubt that he was in no manner a partner with Rasmus. He couldn't be, he was threatened with the loss of all his material possessions, and had already lost the respect of many townspeople.

Perhaps she could win back a little of the respect and trust that she'd lost when he'd found her with Alex at the carriage house. She hadn't yet obtained leave from the Superintendent to reveal her employment, but. . . .

His hands tightened on hers. "I'm sorry you and the children have been caught in the midst of this mess. I can bear it for myself. Giving up the house is no great sacrifice for me. I wouldn't mind living as cheaply as possible for years while paying back the payroll loss. But you and Effie and Evan, you don't deserve this."

She gave him a trembling smile. "Have you forgotten? Even though everything looks hopeless from our viewpoint, God is in control. 'All things work together for good to them that love God.'" She could hear the hesitation in her tear-clogged voice. Why did it make one feel so vulnerable to speak of God? "Isn't that the way the verse reads?"

A small smile tugged at one side of his mouth. "Yes, that's the way it reads."

"When the pastor quoted that verse on the train, I wanted to bounce my pocketbook off his head. I thought it the most ridiculous statement I'd ever heard. But something good did come of our forced marriage. You shared your faith with me. Because of you, I believe in God now. Is there anything greater you could possibly offer me and the children? Surely you don't believe that money or a grand house is of more advantage than faith."

One hand cupped her cheek. The chestnut brown eyes she loved so well glowed as he smiled tenderly down at her.

"You are a wonder, Constance Knight. An absolute wonder."

His touch chased away her breath. It was all she could do to speak.

"Has . . . has the financial situation changed your mind about the annulment?"

The tenderness in his eyes was instantly eliminated by anger. She longed to grab back the hand that dropped from her cheek.

"Still hoping to go back to Alex Bixby? Sorry, but my belief in the sanctity of marriage vows hasn't changed, even if I am sorry to bring my financial problems down on your shoulders."

Resentment charged through her. *How could he be so abominable?* She opened her lips to retort. Clamped them shut. Wounded pride was urging her to build another wall of lies between them. She wouldn't. There had been enough deceit. There would be no more on her part.

The resolution straightened her shoulders. Boldly, she reached for the hands which had only moments before touched her so tenderly. The unexpected move brought Justin's puzzled, still angry eyes to hers.

"I was not thinking of Alexander. I inquired only that I might know whether I dared tell you that . . . that in spite of the 'mess', as you refer to it. . . together we can get by, you and I and the Lord." Her words trailed off.

His fingers crushed hers. The hope in his eyes drove her lashes down in astonishment and wonder. "Do you mean that?"

She nodded, unable to trust her voice to answer his hoarse question.

His hands framed her face, lifting it until she could not help but look into his joy-filled eyes.

Now was the time to tell him she was a Pinkerton agent. Before she lost her courage. She laid her fingers gently on his lips to prevent them from claiming her own. "There's something I must tell you. About. . ."

"Aunt Conthtanthe, I can't find Regina."

They drew apart instantly at Effie's unexpected question.

The little girl stood in her linen nightgown, rubbing her eyes at the lights in the room, her face screwed into a tired pout.

"I thought you were asleep hours ago, dear."

"I woke up and couldn't find my doll."

Constance smoothed the girl's sleep-rumpled hair. "You probably left Regina in my room. Remember you were playing with her on my bed after dinner?"

"I'll go look for Regina with you, Effie." Justin picked the little girl up. He smiled broadly at Constance, the thinly-veiled ardor in his eyes sending her heart tumbling. "I don't want you to get sidetracked, Mrs. Knight. There's one or two things I mean to say to you before you retire. Wait for me here."

Constance waited. The memory of the light in his eyes kept her company. It seemed only moments before she heard him re-enter the library. "Did you find Regina?"

"Yes."

The curtness of his reply stunned her. His face could have been set in granite. What had happened in the few short minutes he'd been gone?

"The doll was lying on your writing desk. Beside this."

He dropped a crumpled piece of her personalized stationery into her lap as though he couldn't stand bear to touch it.

"Sorry it's not in the pristine condition in which I found it."

"Oh!" She didn't have to unwad it to know what it was, the unfinished daily report on the Rasmus Pierce case she was writing for the Superintendent.

Contempt twisted his lips. "I thought you so fine, so pure and trustworthy. And all along you were living in my home under false pretenses. A Pinkerton agent!"

fourteen

"A Pinkerton agent!"

The words echoed off the booklined walls. The scorn in his voice and eyes burned her very soul. "I was going to tell you. . ."

"When the case was over and you were ready for that annulment, I suppose."

"No, it was what I started to tell you when Effie interrupted us."

"Convenient story."

"You must believe me!"

"I shall never believe you again."

"Justin, please, let me explain." The words were a tangled sob.

"Explain? How can you possibly explain choosing such a degrading profession? You must have seen many unsavory situations in your work, been involved with people with whom no decent woman would associate. No wonder you hadn't a problem meeting another man clandestinely while married to me!"

"I told you why I met Alex."

"And the children, how could you expose those sweet kids to the danger inherent in your profession?"

"I never intended them to be exposed to danger. I was simply bringing them to Aunt Libby's. My assignment was to become friendly with Mrs. Pierce and try to obtain information from her regarding Rasmus. The agency didn't even know Rasmus was in the area. We thought he was still in Missouri. It wasn't my fault he robbed the train we boarded. Nor that he insisted we marry."

The muscles in his neck stood out like cords of rope. "Excuses! How could you help but realize you would be putting the children in danger bringing them along while you worked on a case in any capacity?"

He paced four long, sharp paces toward the marble-trimmed fireplace. Four paces back. Glared at her.

"'Everything that deceives may be said to enchant.' Plato said that, in case you've forgotten. He was certainly correct about you. You were completely enchanting. You're very good at deceit. I never suspected you were a detective."

Indignation brought her to her feet, her hands clenched into fists at her sides. "Of course I'm good at my profession! Why shouldn't I be?" Was that her voice, high and shrill? "Why shouldn't I honor the pledge I made to my employer to keep my purpose here secret? Why give criminals advantages they don't give law-abiding citizens? Did Rasmus warn you that he was going to rob the train or the bank?"

"Why did you become a detective?"

"Because I love justice."

"Justice?" His lips twisted in an ugly sneer. "Don't make me laugh."

"Yes, justice. And yes, love for it has put me in many unsavory situations among people with whom you would likely never associate. Do you believe, truly believe, that women should close their eyes and ears to the evils perpetrated in this world? That women should have no part in combating them? Aren't they as often victims as men? Have they no responsibility for sustaining justice?"

"There are other ways women can fight injustice, ways that don't involve deceit. Such as by raising children to love the Lord and goodness."

He grabbed his jacket from the back of a chair and she watched, fuming, as he left the room. A moment later the front door slammed. Was he so angry he'd left the house?

She rushed to the hall, almost tripping over her long skirt.

His favorite hat was missing from the hall rack. Desolation swept over her. He had left, furious at her, despising her.

"Good riddance," she muttered, walking back into the library. She dropped down on the sofa, crossed one leg over the other, swung it back and forth furiously. Stood up. Started pacing.

No use trying to relax. Never had she been so angry. Never had she allowed her temper to break from her control. Never had she yelled at anyone.

She stopped abruptly at the fireplace, ran a finger along the edge of the mantle. "Never have I been so in love, or so afraid," she whispered.

Would he ever let himself trust her again? Living with his contempt would be unbearable. If only she had told him earlier that she was an operative!

She threw herself down on the cool leather of the sofa, cushioning her face in her arms, and sobbed herself to sleep.

It was hours later Constance awoke. She stirred uncomfortably and looked about. The lights were still burning. What had awakened her? She sat up stiffly. Lowered her head into her hands with a groan. Had her crying spell brought on this crushing headache?

The clock in the hallway began chiming the hour. One—two—three—four—five. Five in the morning! It couldn't be.

The back door slammed. *Justin!* Her heart began beating louder than the grandfather clock. If only he would forgive her! She raced down the hall, through the swinging door to the kitchen. A man's figure was silhouetted against the screen door by the light from a battered tin lantern on the rectangular oak table.

He swung around.

Her blood turned to ice. "Rasmus!"

❧

From the end of the dock, Justin stared into the black waters of the Mississippi lapping at the wooden posts. The smell of the river and the sound of its gentle waves were usually soothing when he was battered from life's battles. He found no peace here tonight.

Pain more intense than he'd ever known gripped his heart relentlessly. With a deep groan, he squatted down on the damp wood, plowing his fingers through his hair. His hat fell unheeded to the planks beside him.

Boats steamed past, their lights reflecting in waving paths. The voices of dockmen rose and fell. He was oblivious to it all.

Constance's face filled his mind, with the timid pledge in her eyes as she whispered, "Together we can get by, you and I and the Lord." He'd thought in that moment the Lord had handed him heaven on earth, only to have his heart torn out by the roots minutes later when he found her note.

"Enchantress!" The bitter indictment rent the gentle night breeze.

He hadn't suspected the snags and quicksand and currents that lay beneath the image of the peaceful, strong, compassionate woman. She was only playing a role, one of numerous roles she must have played as a detective. Would he ever know who she really was? Would he ever dare allow himself to trust her again?

He hadn't known betrayal could spiral through a person, burning and piercing all at once, wrapping one in despair and fury. And make the future look as black as that water flowing past.

Is this what Marian experienced when he told her of his marriage to Constance? "Forgive me, Lord, for hurting Marian. Heal her, regardless of the reason. Heal her, and bring to her the good that Thou hast promised to those who love Thee."

Healing. His heart was so raw that healing seemed impossible.

He buried his face in trembling hands. "Lord, I thought if

we honored the vows, this marriage would have Thy blessing. I don't understand why Thou hast allowed our lives to be joined, or why Thou hast allowed me to love Constance beyond reason, when Thou must have known it would bring this pain. I beg that Thou wouldst heal me."

He didn't know how long he sat there, reliving the joy of Constance's presence in his life, the thrill of believing earlier tonight that he'd finally begun to win her love, the fire of knowing he'd been deceived.

The walk home was like walking to his own hanging. Constance would be there. He'd have to see her and speak to her and be constantly reminded of her betrayal. It was more than any man should be expected to endure.

Forgive her.

The words stopped his steps on a street corner near his home. "I can't. It's too soon!"

Constance had been amazed that he would forgive Rasmus. That had been easy compared to forgiving her. He'd never given Rasmus his heart.

But there would be no peace for him without forgiving her. His throat tried to close against the words.

"Lord, help me to forgive her. And please, make our marriage the union Thou dost desire. In Thy Son's name. Amen."

Could they have a real marriage without trust?

Had a light flashed from his parlor window? It must have been his imagination, there was no light there now. Certainly Constance wouldn't be waiting up for him. He shrank from the thought of facing her.

But what if something had happened to the children? How could he have allowed himself to become so wrapped up in self-pity that he had forgotten the need to watch over them?

Fear swamped him as he hurried up the steps, and his heart reached for the Lord with a prayer he didn't know how to put into words.

fifteen

Lantern light flickered grotesquely on the kitchen walls.

"Right the first time, Mrs. Knight. Rasmus Pierce, at yer service." His chuckle raised the hair on the back of her neck. "Or more precisely, yer at my service."

In the light from the battered lantern, his face was gray between his black derby and the thin beard that covered the bottom half of his face. His hair no longer curled over his collar, and the Vandyke beard had been sacrificed to an overall beard. No doubt to better disguise himself from the Pinkerton agents whom he must know were searching for him, Constance thought.

A dark farmer's jacket reached just below his hips, covering a checked flannel shirt tucked into brown corduroy trousers. Her training had recorded her observations of his looks and dress in a moment. What caught her attention were his eyes, and the triumphant look that glittered there. It chilled her to the marrow.

Was he here to harm the children? *Stop that! Get your emotions under control,* she chided herself. *Don't let him know you're frightened. Remember your training.* She took a deep breath, disguising it somewhat by lifting her chin. *Let the breath out slowly. That's better.*

"What may I do for you, Mr. Pierce?"

"For starters, ya kin git inta the parlor, where we'll be more comfortable waitin' fer yer husband."

"My husband hasn't risen yet. Since you are so eager to speak with him, I'll waken him for you."

"Stop right there, Mrs. Knight."

She froze with her hand on the swinging door. Had that brushing sound been a gun being withdrawn from its holster? Why, why had she removed the pocket with her derringer earlier in the evening? She forced herself to turn about, swallowed her heart which had settled in her throat. Rasmus had a pistol leveled at her.

Zeke is in the carriage house, she encouraged herself. *Surely he'll arise soon, and realize something is amiss.*

"I thought you wanted to speak with my husband?"

"It'll be easier ta do when he gits home. Ya see, I know he went out last night and hasn't come back."

"But. . ."

"I told ya on the train thet I have eyes and ears ever'where. If yer expectin' thet man out back ta help ya, ya kin quit yer waitin'. He's tied up pretty as a present."

Obviously no help would be forthcoming from that quarter. At least Zeke was still alive, or Rasmus wouldn't have bothered to tie him up. But there was still Justin, somewhere out in the night.

He moved past her to push open the swinging door with his back. "Lead the way ta the parlor."

She walked slowly down the hall, her heels clipping softly on the marble floor, trying to portray a calmness entirely lacking inside her. If only the children would remain sleeping until—until what? *Please God, protect them!*

She touched a wall button when she entered the parlor, filling the room with brilliant light from the chandelier. Perhaps when Justin returned, he would see Rasmus through the window.

"Douse thet light, pronto!"

"But, Mr. Pierce. . ."

He pushed her away from the wall and punched the switch. The lantern light seemed impossibly dim after the chandelier.

Would the semidarkness hide her movements long enough for her to subdue Rasmus? Only if she managed it before his eyes readjusted to the lantern light. Her knowledge of the room was to her advantage. Her mind cast about for a weapon. The fireplace tools? She started in that direction.

"Hold it. Set down in this here chair."

Disappointment threatened to overwhelm her as she lowered herself into the blue damask-covered rosewood ladies chair. It was nowhere near the fireplace. *Don't think as though you are already defeated,* she shook herself mentally. *Something else must be available. Remember, Pinkerton operatives must be ever ready to take advantage of the most trifling circumstances.*

Rasmus pulled the heavy drapes over the windows. "Don't want the mister seein' the light 'fore he gets inside."

Darkness enveloped her heart. *He mustn't harm Justin!*

He perched on the edge of the grandfather chair opposite her, setting the lantern on the marble-topped table beside him. "Ya try ta git away, and I'll hev ta hurt ya."

Her hand clutched at the neck of her white shirtwaist. "Get away? From one of the country's most dangerous criminals? You credit me with a great deal more courage than I have."

Had her high, squeaky voice fooled him? One of the things she'd learned from watching women on her cases was that their voices invariably rose with fear.

Even in the dim light she could see the grin splitting his beard. "One of the country's most dang'rous crim'nals, huh? I like thet."

He would, with his demented values, she thought.

Rasmus pulled a can of chewing tobacco from his coat pocket, pushed the top off with a dirty thumb. She could barely control a grimace as he stuffed a pinch in his cheek and grinned with stained teeth.

It seemed a decade before Justin's step sounded on the front verandah, though Constance knew from the brass and crystal clock on the mantle that only fifteen minutes had passed. The footfall sent fear and hope spiraling through her together.

Rasmus' derby dropped over the lantern. "Not a sound, Mrs."

The front door opened. A prayer for Justin's safety flew from her heart. Her fingernails cut into the palms of her hands. She forced them open, spreading her fingers along her purple and cream striped skirt. Took a deep breath. She must stay as relaxed as possible.

The sound of the door closing. Footsteps in the hallway. They stopped. Came nearer the parlor.

She opened her mouth to yell. Shut her teeth hard in her lips. With Rasmus armed and expecting him, would her warning further endanger Justin?

"Constance?"

Should she answer his hesitant query?

"And company, Justin." Rasmus lifted the derby, accidentally brushing the box of snuff from the table to the carpet. Light flashed off the barrel of his pistol, which was aimed directly at the door.

"Come in and join us."

He looks awful, she thought when Justin entered. Pity fought with fear in her chest. A day's growth covered his chin. His eyes were black hollows from sleeplessness, his hair rumpled.

She could see his face turning as he searched the room, stop when he recognized her.

"Have they harmed you, Constance?"

"No." She blinked back sudden tears at the repressed anger in his voice. She wished they could see each other better in the lantern light, so he would be more apt to believe her. "Mr. Pierce, now that my husband has returned, may we turn on the lights?"

He rose and hit the button.

The sudden light set spots dancing before her eyes.

"Set yerself down, Justin. No, a little further from the Mrs. Thet's the way," he approved as Justin lowered himself to the edge of the sofa.

Justin's gaze was searching her face as though to prove to himself she had truly not been harmed. *Did he care so much? Did it mean he had forgiven her?* She smiled slightly to reassure him.

His attention shifted to Rasmus. "What's this all about?"

"Heard ya have a proposition ta make me," Rasmus said around the tobacco forming a ball in his cheek.

Constance stifled a gasp. Where had Rasmus heard that? The announcement hadn't appeared in the newspaper yet.

Justin didn't show any surprise at Rasmus' knowledge. "That's right. A compromise."

Rasmus leaned back until the grandfather chair creaked and stood protesting on its back legs. "Let's hear it."

"A good deal of the money you stole from the express car was mine. $70,000 of the money you took from the bank was payroll for one of the local log mills."

"Read 'bout the payroll in the paper. Glad ta hear I did ya out of a might on the train, too." His shoulders shook in a chuckle.

Justin waited for his mirth to cease. "This is the proposition. You keep the money that belonged to me, and return the rest. In exchange, the bank, express company, and railroad will drop all charges against you and your men."

Rasmus' bark of a laugh cut off abruptly. The front legs of his chair dropped to the thick carpet with a soft thud. "Ya think yer the only ones lookin' fer us? Why, even the Mrs. here knows I'm one of the most dangerous men in the country. What do I care if'n charges are dropped fer a couple of measly strikes? Won't stop ever'one chasin' me."

"People in *this* area would stop, and they'd have a softer spot in their hearts for you. After all, until now, you've never been known to steal from your former neighbors and your parents' customers and friends."

"Friends! As if anyone gives my folks the time of day 'cept

fer people curious 'bout me."

"That's not true!" Constance interrupted eagerly. "Your parents are well liked and respected. At least they were until you blew the express car."

"Oh yeah? An' what would a little lady like yerself know 'bout it?" With an oath, he jerked to his feet. "No more 'bout my folks from either of ya. I've listened to yer offer, Knight. Now ya listen ta mine. Those two little kids been livin' here, some of my pals took 'em out of here 'bout two hours ago."

"No!" The word exploded from Constance's lips, terror whipping through her.

Justin bolted from the sofa.

"Stop right there, Knight!"

Justin stopped at the sight of the pistol leveled at him, the muscles in his cheeks working, hands clenched menacingly at his sides. "If you've harmed those youngsters. . ."

Was her face as pale as his beneath his stubble? It felt like it. She was hot and cold and lightheaded all at once. *"All things work together for good to them that love God,"* she reminded herself silently. *Surely that promise is for children like Effie and Evan, also. It had to be!*

Yellowed teeth showed in Rasmus' beard. "Didn't think we'd get 'em out of here without wakin' the Mrs. from her nap in the lib'ary. My men had jest started down the street with 'em when she found me in the kitchen."

This couldn't be happening. Was he bluffing? Perhaps the children were still in their beds.

"You mentioned an offer. What is it?" Fury filled Justin's words. His face was so rigid it was a wonder he could speak at all.

"Ya give me five thousand dollars, and I give ya back the kids."

Constance gasped.

Justin glanced at her and back to Rasmus. "I haven't the

money. You've taken everything. My investments have been liquidated to pay for this house, or a portion of it."

The grin slithered across Rasmus' face again, broader than ever. His eyes glittered. "No kiddin'! I've made the great Justin Knight a poor man?"

"A tough man like you doesn't need to hide behind a couple of children, Rasmus."

"Nope. But I'm not ag'inst raisin' money on anythin' I can, kids included."

"I told you, I haven't any money."

Rasmus waved his free hand. "But there's all this. A fine house, horses, and carriages. Should be able to raise 'nough cash fer the kids. If not," his shoulders lifted the dark canvas jacket in a shrug, "I'll keep 'em for comp'ny fer Marian, leastwise 'til they git on my nerves."

"Think Marian would still agree to become your wife if she finds you stoop to stealing children?"

At Justin's sneering comment, all semblance of patience dropped from Rasmus' face. His voice sent white fear slithering along Constance's veins. "We wouldn't of taken the kids at all if'n ya'd kept yer word. Marian said ya told her 'bout yer weddin', an' she was breakin' our engagement. But she promised ta marry me, and she's goin' ta marry me."

"Planning to kidnap her, like you did the children?"

"No need ta, banker. She's already at my place."

"Not by her choice, I'm sure."

"It will be her choice, 'ventually."

"You're wrong, Rasmus. You can't force people to love you."

Didn't Justin know better than to goad him? Anger was turning the man's face purple.

"Don't need no sermons from you, Knight." He pointed the gun at Constance, setting her skin crawling. "You, git over here with me. Goin' ta be daylight soon, I got ta git ridin'. The Mrs. will be goin' long fer pertection. Spot anyone on our trail, she's dead." He frowned at Constance. "What ya waitin' fer? I said git over here."

She rose shakily to her feet. Slowly she began walking. She sunk her top teeth hard into her bottom lip. *Think, Constance! There has to be a way out. There always is, one only has to recognize it.*

Rasmus spat his tobacco wad out the side of his mouth unto the carpet. "Move it, woman!"

The tobacco!

With a swift, graceful move, she knelt to pick up the can of chewing tobacco that had been knocked to the floor. Thank the Lord not much had fallen from the can. Could Rasmus hear the exultant beating of her heart?

She held the can in her palm as she rose. "You dropped this." Her breath stopped. She'd only have one chance.

He snorted a laugh. "Quite a lady you married, Knight. Even polite when she's bein'. . ."

She tossed the tobacco directly into Rasmus' face.

sixteen

Rasmus clutched at his eyes with his free hand, swearing liberally.

"Git it off! It burns! Git it off!"

Justin lurched for the outlaw, knocking the pistol from his hand. It fired upon landing at her feet. Her courage nearly failed her as she felt the wind of the bullet whiz past her ear. A moment later she grabbed the gun and trained it on the struggling men.

"Sit down, Pierce!" Amazing that her voice wasn't shaking like laundry in a windstorm.

Still swearing, Pierce dropped to the floor with tears streaming in rivulets through tobacco on his cheeks.

"There's some rope in the pantry." Justin disappeared and was back in a minute that seemed like a year.

She'd been taught to shoot a variety of firearms, but she wasn't accustomed to handling them for any period of time. Her wrists were protesting severely by the time Justin had Rasmus secured hand and foot.

"Where's Zeke?"

"Rasmus said he was tied up in the carriage house." She lowered the gun, but didn't put it down. One thing she had learned well through the years was not to trust any criminal, even those who appeared harmless.

She glanced quickly at Justin and back to Rasmus. "Do you think he was bluffing about the children? Could they still be in bed?"

He was out of the room before she finished speaking. His feet pounded up the stairs and down the upper hallway. They didn't pound on his way back down.

"Not there," was his terse statement when he re-entered the room.

Rasmus stubbornly refused to tell them where Marian and the children were being held. Constance was thankful for the years of experience as an agent that helped her keep her emotions from spinning out of control at worry for the children. She could only be a help to them if she kept calm.

Finally they gave up questioning Rasmus, and Justin rang up the sheriff.

While he used the telephone, Constance released Zeke, whose black and blue eye distinguished the effort he'd made against capture.

When they arrived back in the house, Justin was just hanging up the telephone, and she asked whether Sheriff Tucker would be coming for Rasmus.

"No. Zeke and I will be taking him to the jail house." He turned his attention to Zeke. "Bixby was with the sheriff when I rang up. The plan is for you to gather the agents in town. Some will stay with you and the deputies to guard the jail in case Rasmus' pals hear of his arrest and try to spring him. Bixby and I and the rest of the agents will form a posse and join Sheriff Tucker in searching outlying farmhouses and abandoned buildings once more. I'll be ready to go as soon as I change."

While Justin changed clothes, Constance changed too, exchanging her purple and cream striped skirt and purple bolero vest for a blue serge divided skirt and matching Eton jacket, the better for horseback riding. The flap that disguised the trouserlike aspect of the skirt would also serve to hide the pocket carrying her derringer. She would not be caught without the weapon again.

She was waiting in the hallway when Justin came out of his bedchamber. He'd changed to a flannel shirt, courdoroys, and boots, but hadn't taken time to shave.

"I'm going with you."

"Like fun, you are." He brushed past her.

She grabbed his flannel sleeve. "Effie and Evan are my niece and nephew, not yours. I'm the Pinkerton operative, not you. You have no right to keep me from joining you."

"I have the right of a husband, or perhaps you've forgotten." His eyes scorched her.

Her cheeks burned. "I've forgotten nothing. But I'll not sit here and knit while you look for the children."

His hands clasped her shoulders, crushing the pert pleated sleeves. "When I came home and found Rasmus here. . ." His voice cracked and he pressed his lips fervently to her temple. "Don't you know how thankful I am you weren't harmed or killed?"

The gravelly words whispered into her hair sent waves of hope through her.

He cleared his throat and pulled away far enough to look into her face. "It will be difficult enough keeping my mind clear of my fear for the children. I won't have the added distraction of your safety. Either you agree to stay here, or I shall lock you in your room."

"You wouldn't dare!"

"Wouldn't I?"

The challenge in his eyes and voice answered that question.

"Will you stay?" he demanded.

"What choice have you given me?"

Couldn't he understand that she didn't want to worry about his safety any more than he wanted to worry about hers? Why did men think the more valiant part of courage lay in fighting, and not in waiting and praying while your heart burned itself out in worry and fear and love? But how could she admit her fear for him when such an abyss of problems lay between them?

His grip loosened and his voice gentled. "Will you include

me in your prayers while you wait? I've no doubt your heart has been sending forth prayers for the children since the moment we heard of their abduction, as has mine."

She blinked back the tears that suddenly threatened. "Of course."

He turned to go.

She clutched his sleeve. Her recent hope washed away when she saw his eyes. How could they be so cold and remote, after those words, after that kiss? They almost frightened her from asking, but she had to know. "Is. . .is there anything I can offer God that will make Him more likely to answer my prayers for Effie and Evan?"

"You mean, to make a bargain with Him?"

She nodded, her lips clamped hard in her teeth.

"No. We cannot bargain with God."

"Do you think God would allow something awful to happen to the twins because. . .because I wasn't forthcoming with you about my position with the Pinkerton agency?"

"No!" She cringed at the thundered word, and his face twisted. With a shuddering sigh, he cupped her cheek with one hand. "You mustn't torture yourself with such a thought. The Bible tells us God is love. Would love harm two little children for the purpose of punishing you?"

"I suppose not."

"Of course not. I don't know why He allows some of the hard things. I can't guarantee Effie's and Evan's safety. But their abduction is not God's way of punishing you."

"Thank you."

At her muffled whisper, he dropped his hand.

There was one more request she *must* make before he left. If anything happened to either of them. . . .

"Please." She allowed all the yearning in her heart to fill the word.

He hesitated at the top of the stairs, his wary gaze locked with hers.

"Please forgive me for deceiving you."

His gaze didn't falter. He didn't blink. A muscle tightened in his cheek. "I already have. But forgiveness doesn't restore trust."

And then he was gone.

She stood transfixed, listening to his footsteps recede, not wanting to believe his words. Would her chest continue burning for the rest of her life?

Dashing tears from her lashes, she hurried downstairs. She must be about her plan. It was the children's safety that mattered, not her justly battered heart.

From the back door, she watched Justin mount his favorite riding horse, a huge black, and ride off to meet the posse. As soon as he was out of sight, she dashed to the barn and saddled a small roan.

She rode quickly down to Pierce's Store, securing the roan at the back of the building. She didn't want to chance identification of either herself or the horse if Justin came by with the posse.

As usual, Mrs. Pierce was alone in the store when Constance entered. There was no welcoming smile on her face, only the spine-chilling reservation of hopelessness. Constance was certain she'd already heard of her son's arrest.

Mrs. Pierce stood silently, waiting for Constance to speak, the palms of her hands sliding idly up and down the blue cotton apron covering her hips. Constance resisted the impulse to take those hands in hers and quiet them. Strange, she almost felt guilty for having a part in the arrest of her son.

"I'm sorry, Mrs. Pierce."

The narrow, gray-topped head nodded once, slowly. The woman's eyes never left Constance's, but there was no accusation in them.

"They say he was arrested at your home. That you and your husband overpowered him."

"Yes."

"Well, it had to happen sometime. Seems I've been waitin' for it since he was a kid." Her chin trembled. "They're sayin' he stole your kids, Evan and that pretty little girl."

"Yes." Relief sighed in the admission. She'd been wondering how she was going to interrupt the woman's grief to introduce her own. Mrs. Pierce was the only one who could and would help them find the children, she was certain. There was little chance the posse would locate the hideout that had so long eluded local law enforcement and the Pinkertons.

"I'm that mortified over his takin' them that I can hardly think to work. What you must be goin' through, worryin' about them!"

"As a woman and mother, of course you must understand my concern."

The door to the back room closed with a soft thud, and they turned toward it. Mr. Meeker, wide-brimmed hat in his hands, was racing up the rickety stairs to the second floor.

Constance turned back. "I came for your assistance."

Iron-gray eyebrows peaked in surprise. "Help from me?"

"Yes." She lifted a quick prayer for guidance. "You have probably heard that a posse has been organized to find the children, and Marian Ames, whom your son is also having held against her will."

"Miss Marian?"

She couldn't let herself be sidetracked by the woman's apparent shock.

"If the posse locates your son's hideout, people on both sides of the law are apt to be hurt, possibly killed. That would only make things worse for Rasmus."

Why did the woman keep glancing at the back of the store? Constance wanted to shake her bony shoulders and make her pay attention. "Mrs. Pierce, I'm sure you don't wish the children's and Marian's lives endangered any more than I. Should they be harmed, Rasmus is certain to receive the harshest punishment. But if the men with whom he was associated can be taken peaceably, and the stolen money retrieved, perhaps the law will be more lenient."

Mrs. Pierce lowered herself slowly to the top of a barrel beside the counter, glanced again at the back of the store. Bony fingers fidgeted with the tiny black bow at the neck of her plain gray dress.

"Why come to me?"

"I think you know where your son has been staying."

The washed-out blue eyes swung back to observe her, but she didn't reply.

"I can understand that as his mother you couldn't betray his hiding place earlier. But he's behind bars now and there's nothing further to be gained for him by keeping his secret." Her voice had broken on that last sentence. My word, she wasn't going to break down and cry, was she? She couldn't afford to give in to such emotionalism now, of all times, when Effie and Evan's safety depended upon her!

Footsteps pounded down the stairs. Mr. Pierce was settling an old gray hat on his head. "I'm goin' with Meeker, Ma."

Mrs. Pierce started up from the barrel, her hands out pleadingly. "Pa, no. . .!"

"Don't know when I'll get back," was his only response before the two men left through the back entry.

Constance wouldn't have thought it possible that the woman's face could have grown grayer. What had happened that she hadn't seen? Two men leaving. . . . Could it be, was it possible that Mr. Meeker was connected with Rasmus' gang? But he'd only moved to the area recently! Still, stranger things had happened.

She grasped Mrs. Pierce's arm. "Where are they going?"

"I . . . I'm not certain."

"*Please*! You are the only one who can help Marian and the children!"

The woman stared at the door where she'd last seen her husband. After a few tense moments, she squared her thin shoulders beneath the gray dress. A strange peace softened the lines in her face.

"Rasmus' men are stayin' at Meeker's place."

"Thank you!" She darted for the door.

"Mrs. Knight!"

She looked over her shoulder, impatient at the interruption.

"I'll go with you. I know where his farm is. Besides, you'd have difficulty gettin' the men to listen to you. They know me."

Constance hurried back to take the woman's shoulders in her hands and smile into her old face. "If a mother's love can do anything to undo the sins of her children, your love is doing so today. Thank you."

"I'll have to get a horse at the livery."

"I'll ring Zeke at the jail house and tell him where we are going. I will meet you at the livery."

Zeke didn't care for her plans, but she didn't tell him where she was calling from. She knew she and Mrs. Pierce would be on their way before he could stop them.

Constance had difficulty keeping her fears at bay as she followed Mrs. Pierce. She tried to ignore the aching in her chest, tried to clear her mind of all the frightening possibilities. She had to keep her wits about her, as Alexander would say.

They didn't take the main road. Mrs. Pierce insisted the back road would be quicker with the horses.

"Likely we'll get there before Pa and Mr. Meeker. Meeker's wagon will slow them up a might. 'Sides, they won't want to arouse suspicions by travelin' fast."

Mrs. Pierce would make a good operative herself, Constance thought.

Along the way Mrs. Pierce told how Meeker had carried messages between Rasmus and his parents. Meeker and his bride had moved to the area a year ago, no one here had any reason to suspect he had ridden with Rasmus in Missouri. Meeker didn't want his bride to know of his criminal association, so when he married and purchased the farm, Rasmus and the others kept their distance. But when Meeker's wife returned to Missouri to care for her ailing mother at the same time Rasmus and his men needed a good local hideout, Meeker offered his farm.

The farmyard was quiet when they reached it. They rode straight into the yard with no attempt to hide and tied their horses to the porch rail.

One of Rasmus' men met them at the door. He was tall with a lean face, a shaggy mustache, and stubble at least two days old. The suspenders holding up his baggy corduroys slipped over the shoulders of his dirty, collarless shirt. He carried a rifle, but greeted Mrs. Pierce with a smile.

"Never 'xpected to see you here, ma'am." The smile faded. "Guess you heard 'bout your boy."

"Yes, Tom."

"Don't you worry none. The boys are on their way to get him out a there."

"Why would they do a fool thing like that?"

"Ma'am?"

"Least in prison, I don't need to worry about his gettin' shot up."

"Now, ma'am, Rasmus ain't goin' to get shot. That one has the luck of the gods, he has."

"Hmph! Can see this discussion is goin' nowhere. And you can quit looking at this lady like she's an ice cream soda. She's married to Justin Knight."

Tom's mouth dropped open and snapped shut. "Mrs. Knight! Not the woman who married him on the train? The woman that. . ."

Constance nodded. "Yes, that woman."

"Well, Tom, where are Miss Ames and the two youngsters Rasmus had brought here?"

Tom glanced warily from Mrs. Pierce to Constance and back again. "Uh, I'm not sure Rasmus would like me sayin'."

"Don't be a fool. How would I know they were here if my son didn't tell me?" She stepped past him and started for a shut door. "Are they in the parlor here?"

"Well, yes'm, but. . ."

"Come along, Mrs. Knight."

They had barely stepped through the door when Effie threw herself against Constance's skirt. "Aunt Conthtanthe! I knew you'd come!"

Evan was close behind. His fingers clutched her skirt and didn't let go, though his eyes met hers fearlessly. "We've been here a long time," he said accusingly.

Constance knelt to hug them both, trying hard to keep back the tears that threatened to form in her eyes and throat. "I know, dears. Say hello to Mrs. Pierce."

They didn't let go of her while they greeted the older woman. Constance used the time to glance about the room. It was furnished simply, with a braided wool rug in the midst of an astonishing variety of cheap furniture. Chromos of flowers and dogs and kittens hung against the cabbage-rose patterned wallpaper. Marian sat on the round stool in front of an ornate parlor organ, her eyes wide.

In one corner, a man sat in a chair upholstered in wine plush. A rifle stood against the wall beside him. A pistol pointed directly at Constance was propped casually on his corduroy covered knees. The sight of it set fright slithering like an eel down her throat and into her stomach. After all these years, she'd never grown accustomed to looking into the 'business end of a pistol,' as Alexander often stated it. And with the children in the room. . . .

The man himself was the opposite of Tom. The dim light

from the simple, two-shaded gas ceiling fixture gleamed softly off his bald head. His neat mustache seemed too small for his fat face. His red collarless shirt strained past the stomach falling over the top of his trousers.

Constance didn't like his eyes. They were beady and small and she hadn't seen them blink once since she entered the room. He was going to be far more difficult to reason with than Tom.

She felt Tom stop inches behind her. "Guess you know Mrs. Pierce, Gent. This here's Justin Knight's wife."

Gent! Gentleman Jake. She should have recognized him. Although his Bertillon card back in Chicago showed him dressed as a dandy. Her heart sank a little. He'd be even more difficult to convince than she'd originally thought.

He removed a fat cigar from his mouth. Keeping his eyes on Constance, he addressed Mrs. Pierce. "You know Rasmus wouldn't want you out here. 'Tisn't safe for a lady like yourself."

"Don't talk patronizin' to me, Gent. Guess I can be here if I want. When Rasmus takes to holdin' women and children against their will, it's time somebody steps in."

"Now, ma'am, don't get riled."

"I've come to take Miss Ames and the youngsters home."

"You know we can't let you do that, ma'am."

"I'm doin' it just the same."

With one quick move of his fat thumb, Gent cocked the pistol. Constance felt her eyes grow wide and the eel slipped down her throat again. She hugged the children closer.

Gent's words were terrifyingly unhurried. "No, ma'am, I'm afraid you're not."

seventeen

She would be reliving this scene in her mind's eye for the rest of her days, Constance thought. The pistol in Gent's flabby hand could wreck the lives of each person in that room.

"Hmpf!" Mrs. Pierce threw back her scrawny shoulders. "There isn't a man in this gang that would have the spunk to shoot me and face Rasmus."

Constance stared at her. She was magnificent! And very probably correct. The thought restored her hope and reason.

Behind her, Tom shifted from one foot to the other.

"What do you think, Gent? Should we let 'em go?"

"Now what do you think Rasmus would say when he gets back here if he found Miss Ames and the children gone? Use your head, Tom."

Mrs. Pierce propped her fists on her skinny hips. "Now you listen to me, Gent. It's my son in prison, and I'm not so sure as you are that he's goin' to get out anytime soon. I don't intend on his facin' the law for abductin' females and youngsters."

"Seems like that should be his choice, ma'am."

"Hogwash. I said I'm takin' these people with me, and I'm takin' them and that's that."

"Mrs. Pierce, I reckon you're right about me not shooting you," Gent drawled. "But I don't think Rasmus would mind if I played target practice with one of these kids, or Mrs. Knight."

Mrs. Pierce whirled around. "No way to sic the law on a person faster than hurtin' women and children."

Gent rolled his cigar around with his tongue. Shoved it to one corner of his mouth.

"I'm getting mighty tired of this discussion. Suppose you sit down somewhere and make yourself comfortable. Because I promise you, none of you are going anywhere."

His voice was too smooth, too devoid of emotion. It was now he'd be at his most dangerous, Constance thought, if her knowledge of people gained from similar situations was any barometer. She touched Mrs. Pierce's arm.

"Let's sit down on that sofa. Mr. Gent's patience seems to be wearing thin."

The older woman pressed her lips together until they almost disappeared, but she followed Constance to the sofa. The children tagged along, still clutching Constance's skirt.

Evan climbed up on Constance's lap, and Effie leaned against the blue serge divided skirt covering her knee. Why, the twins were still in their nightclothes, she realized with a start.

"The men are mean, Aunt Conthtanthe. I dropped Regina, and they wouldn't pick her up. And they pointed gunth at uth."

"But we remembered what Justin told us," Evan said, his brown eyes serious.

Constance smiled at him. "What was that, dear?"

"He told us we're stronger than mean men, because Jesus lives in our hearts, and He's stronger than mean men. Don't you remember?"

"Yes, dear, I remember now."

"We prayed for them, like Justin told us."

"But when we prayed and athked God to make him good, that fat man jutht got madder."

Constance gaze darted to Gent. Had the children prayed aloud for him and Tom and the others? No wonder he'd been angry. *What is more infuriating than to hear a child point out your sins?*

The wooden clock on the paisley, gold-fringed cloth covering the top of the organ showed an hour had passed before Marian crossed the room and sank to the floor beside Constance. Her sapphire and gold striped skirt spread around her in a sunburst of color, though its wrinkles bore evidence of days of wear.

"Have you been treated well?" Constance asked in a low voice.

Marian nodded. "No one laid a hand on me or the children. They just refuse to let us leave."

"Marian wath kind to uth."

Marian smiled slightly and laid a hand on Effie's head. "And Effie and Evan have been kind to me. They've reminded me of some important things today."

Effie leaned harder against Constance's knee and whispered loudly, "Don't you think Marian ith pretty?"

Lovely color tinged Marian's cheeks and jealousy stabbed through Constance. "Very pretty." Justin couldn't help but think so, also. Could a man who had been attracted to Marian's delicate, golden beauty ever find her own dark looks attractive? What did her looks matter? He didn't trust her. Could love exist without trust?

Constance shoved at the desolation threatening to overwhelm her. If she allowed herself to dwell in that emotional quicksand, she and the children might never leave here alive.

She urged Effie and Evan to sit with Mrs. Pierce for a few minutes.

"I think she could use some hugs." Besides, the closer they were to Mrs. Pierce, the safer they were. As the woman had said, Gent and Tom wouldn't want to chance hitting Rasmus' mother.

When the children had transferred their attention to the older woman, Constance turned back to Marian.

"Thank you for trying to comfort them today."

Marian shook her head. "They were braver than I." She took a deep breath. "This is the third day I've been here. I've had a lot of time to think. I don't know how or when we might leave here, or even if we will, but there's some things I must say to you."

"To me?"

She nodded, lifting her delicate features a trifle higher. "I should never have become engaged to Justin. I've always liked him, and was flattered he asked me to marry him, but I wasn't in love with him."

"Please, you owe me no apology."

The blonde woman shook her head vigorously. "I must tell you. Until Justin told me of his marriage to you, I thought my life was almost perfect. I was betrothed to the town's wealthiest bachelor, all my friends envied me, God seemed to be giving me everything I wanted, and demanding little in return. And then you and Justin married, and life became unbearable."

"I'm sorry."

Marian ignored her interruption. "I tried to hurt Justin by agreeing to marry Rasmus, but I only hurt myself. . .and them." She nodded at Effie and Evan, who were carrying on quite a conversation with Mrs. Pierce. "When I discovered the true reason for your marriage, I foolishly flung my knowledge in Rasmus' face. How could I have been so silly as to think a nineteen-year-old girl would be any match for a hardened criminal like Rasmus?"

Constance didn't know what to say. She laid a hand on Marian's shoulder, and the girl continued.

"Listening to the children ask God to forgive these men, I realized how much I've taken God for granted over the years. When I was Effie's and Evan's age, I trusted Him as they do. Anyway, shortly before you arrived, I asked God to forgive me for becoming so self-centered, and recommitted my life to Him."

Constance's heart gave a little leap. Another good thing that had come from her strange marriage to Justin!

"I'm so glad."

Marian clasped one of Constance's hands tight in her own. Blue eyes met green ones. "I don't know how you feel about Justin. I can't imagine being forced to marry as you were. But Justin is a good man. If you decide to stay with him, I hope you will be very happy, and never waste a moment feeling guilty about me."

Constance pressed the girl's fingers. "Thank you."

Marian flushed and pulled her hand away self-consciously. "Oh!" She reached back to touch Constance's wedding ring. "What a lovely band."

Embarrassment heated Constance's cheeks. "I've felt a hypocrite each time I looked at it. It should have been yours."

Marian's curls bounced as she shook her head. "That isn't the ring Justin bought for me. I know, because he asked me to accompany him to select my ring." She turned around and rested her head against the sofa.

Constance glanced at the simple band with the delicate orange blossom design. Had he truly selected it just for her? She touched her lips to it softly. *Thank You, Lord*, her heart rejoiced.

Poor Marian. She might not love Justin, but she had endured a great deal because of Rasmus' love for her. The guilt that had hounded Constance since she first met Marian swept over her. In spite of Justin's love for truth and her own questions regarding the ethics of using deceit to obtain a "noble" end, she could forgive herself for deceiving criminals. But had her deceit hurt others, like Marian? She'd gone merrily on her way after each case was completed, not once looking back to see if her actions had brought harm or sorrow to the innocent.

Marian shifted her position and groaned. "We may never get out of this room."

Constance darted a glance at Tom, still leaning against the door to the hall, and then at Gent in the plush velvet chair. "You mustn't think in such a manner," she urged in a low voice. "Pray, and keep your eyes and ears open. Who knows what opportunities God may give us?"

Marian nodded, but Constance didn't see any hope in her tired, drawn face.

In spite of the few hours sleep she'd had the night before, Constance wasn't tired. She was too nervous and frightened to be tired.

Justin hadn't slept at all. Was he tired now, or was he as wide-eyed as she was? Where was he? Had the posse come across the men attempting to free Rasmus? Had Justin been caught in a gunfight? Her heart twisted at the thought of him, of his beautiful chestnut brown eyes, the rich low laugh she loved, his steady commitment to the Lord, the loving way he'd taken responsibility for the children, his loyalty to the townspeople in spite of the way they'd treated him after he married her.

Would she ever have a chance to tell him that she loved him? Would he care to have her love? Would she ever again feel the touch of his hand on her cheek, or his lips against hers?

Constance sat up a little straighter and folded her hands in her lap. She was going to do everything in her power to see him again!

"Excuse me, Tom."

He jerked his surprised gaze to her and stood straighter.

"What will happen if your friends are unable to free Rasmus, and are themselves apprehended?"

Gent snorted. "Sheriff Tucker couldn't catch a rat in a trap."

Constance gave him her sweetest smile. "I'm sure you know the man's abilities better than I. I've only been in River's Edge for a fortnight or so."

She turned her attention back to Tom, easily the most gullible of the two. Dividing the enemy would give her more advantage. She opened her eyes wider to give Tom her most innocent look. "But suppose, for the sake of argument, that your friends were apprehended. What if they told where you are staying? If the Sheriff found you and Gent here with the children and we three ladies, wouldn't you two be accused of abducting us, rather than Rasmus? Surely no one would believe that Rasmus had his own mother forcibly detained."

From the corner of her eye, she could see Gent hitch forward.

"Shut your mouth, woman!"

Tom shuffled his feet again. His lean face crumpled into a mass of furrows. "She makes sense to me, Gent. Mebbe we should let 'em leave."

"I'll do the thinking around here. Can't you tell she's goading us?"

"I don't know. Mebbe. . ."

"You in the house!"

The holler from outside brought instant stillness to the room.

"Justin!"

Constance didn't need Marian's whisper to know it had been Justin's voice. *Lord, help us. Keep Justin and the children safe. Show us what to do.*

Grunting, Gent pushed himself from the chair and crashed against the wall beside a window, trying to make his round body flat.

Tom slipped to another window.

Effie and Evan hurried back to Constance.

"That's Justin," Evan announced.

Constance nodded and put a finger to her lips.

"We know you're in there."

Justin again. Constance's heart started tripping at another level. God had at least kept him safe until now.

"There's a posse of twelve armed men out here, mostly Pinkerton agents. We don't want trouble. We just want the women and children released."

Tom's face was deathly pale against the cabbage roses on the wallpaper.

"Pinks, Gent!"

"Shut up." Gent swung the barrel of his pistol against the glass. Constance heard the tinkle of it falling.

"You want them?" Gent hollered, his fat chin wobbling. "You come get them!"

eighteen

Gent's holler reverberated through the room.

Constance slipped her hand into the pocket beneath the panel of her split skirt, grasped the pearl handle of her derringer. Her gaze was glued on Gent. She opened her mouth to tell the children to get down.

Gent poked his pistol barrel out the broken window and fired before she could speak.

She was vaguely aware of Marian dragging Evan to the floor. She reached for Effie, but was hindered by her pocket.

Horror held her motionless, her mouth went desert dry, watching Effie tear across the braided rug toward Gent in her linen nightshirt and bare feet, her curls flying.

A moment later Constance was on her feet, the derringer pulled from her pocket. But by then, Effie's fists were pummeling Gent's stomach, her high little voice screeching furiously. "Don't you dare shoot Juthtin! Don't you dare!"

Constance felt as though she was moving through molasses. Terror tumbled through her. Would she be able to stop Gent in time?

He turned with a bellow, pulled back his arm as though to strike the child with his pistol. He mustn't harm her!

A sound rang out. A vibration ran up her arm. The pistol dropped from Gent's hand and his bellow increased.

Had she fired the shot?

A loud thud came from behind her, but she didn't dare turn around. Gent was diving for his pistol, grasping for it with his good hand. If he reached it. . . . Her derringer was no good, it only held one shot.

161

"Move away, Effie!" Her voice finally worked.

Effie ignored her and stomped her heel into Gent's injured hand. Howling, he forgot the weapon and huddled over his hand.

Constance shoved Effie out of the way, kicked Gent's pistol from his reach, and hurried to retrieve it. She swung around, pointing it at the groaning, swearing man. He glared at her with pain-glazed eyes.

She glanced around. Mrs. Pierce had Tom's rifle in her arms, pointed at Tom, who was lying on the floor. Had that been the thud she'd heard?

Evan was still with Marian on the floor beside the sofa. Effie was leaning against a chair, panting from her efforts.

Suddenly she recalled the men outside, that shouts and a smattering of shots had filled the background during the storm they'd been through in this room. Had anyone outside been hurt by the one shot Gent had gotten off?

Careful to stay out of Gent's reach, she leaned close to the window and called, "Come into the parlor, gentlemen. We have some gifts for you."

≈

Constance watched the last of the posse leave, taking Tom and Gent with them. Mrs. Pierce accompanied them. Would she lean on God during this difficult time? Constance hoped so.

Resting her hand on the side of the organ, she surveyed the small room. What would Mrs. Meeker think when she returned from her mother's to find her husband in jail and her home the sight of a gunfight? She wished she could spare the woman the pain of her husband's betrayal.

Had Justin felt as betrayed when he found she was a Pinkerton operative? She'd almost hoped he was learning to love her, until he made that discovery. Would he ever let himself love her now?

He hadn't spoken to her since entering the room, but his eyes had slashed at her more sharply than knives ever could.

Even now his back was turned to her, his anger dividing them more effectively than the space between them. The children were demanding all his attention, and he was squatting before them, listening to their eager tale. Even with Justin's resentment tearing her heart to ribbons, she was overwhelmingly grateful to the Lord for keeping him safe.

Alexander moved away from Marian and Mrs. Pierce toward Justin and the twins. "Aren't you two going to let old Uncle Alex in on your stories?"

They turned their attention to him eagerly. After a minute, Justin turned to face her. Anger still stood plain on his face, so hot she was certain it would melt her.

He came toward her slowly. She tried to tear her gaze from his, but it was as though they were cemented together. Her chest ached with her held breath. She would have retreated if she weren't already against the wall.

"I told you to stay at home." Fury cracked like a whip in his low voice. "When Zeke caught up with us after the attempt to free Rasmus was squelched and told us you were headed here with Mrs. Pierce. . ." Both hands plowed through his hair. "How could you have done such a foolish thing?"

Marian's beaming face was suddenly beside him. "What the man is trying to say, with a gentleman's usual finesse, is that he was terrified you would be harmed, and he doesn't know how to express his joy at your safety."

Justin's face flushed. "I said exactly what I meant."

Marian jerked at his arm with her dainty hands until he scowled at her.

"Justin Knight, you're a fool. You have no call to be so angry with Constance. You should be thanking God for such a courageous wife. Why, she married you, a stranger, and went to live with you in order to save your life and the children's. How did she know you were a gentleman? You could as easily have been a reprobate. Don't bother protesting, you could have been, for all she knew. And today she risked her life to save not only the children, but her husband's former fiancee and the mother of the man who forced her to marry a stranger. If you cannot appreciate what an extraordinary woman you've married, well, you don't deserve her."

"That's telling him," Alex called laughingly from across the room.

Justin glared at him. "I'd appreciate it if you two allowed my wife and I to work out our own affairs."

Constance's heart gave a little leap at his words. Did that mean that he *wanted* to work things out between them?

"Yes, sir," Marian said with exaggerated meekness. Her brow furrowed. "How did you know where to find us?"

Justin dug his hands into the pockets of his corduroys. "We found Effie's doll a couple miles down the road, just about the time Meeker and Mr. Pierce came by in Meeker's wagon. Didn't take a Pinkerton agent to figure out this was a likely place to look."

Effie swung about, eyes wide. "You found Regina?"

Justin nodded, his face softening. "She's in my saddlebag."

"Ooooh! Thank you!"

Evan's serious eyes looked up at him from beside Alex.

"Will you take us to Pirate's Cave, Justin?"

"Pirate's Cave?"

"You said you played there when you were little like us. Gent said Rasmus put loot there." The round face puckered into furrows of curiosity. "What's loot?"

"They must have stored the stolen money in the cave!"

Excitement snapped in Alex's eyes. "You know where this cave is located?"

"I could find it in my sleep. It's in the bluffs above the river between here and River's Edge."

Alex was on his feet instantly. "Then we can recover it on the way back to town."

It was all Constance and Marian could do to keep the children from joining the men in their search when they reached the bluffs where they'd picnicked their first Sunday in River's Edge. Constance's heart lodged in her throat while she watched the men descend the gray cliffs. But it wasn't long before they were back with bags and gunnysacks filled with money and bonds, which they piled in the bed of a wagon borrowed from Meeker's farm.

When they returned to town, they all went first to Justin's home. The group was barely off their horses and out of the wagon before Aunt Libby and Mrs. Kelly rushed across the lawn, followed by a short, stocky man in a brown checked suit, with round wire-rimmed glasses perched on his short nose, holding a pencil in one hand and a notebook in the other.

Justin's jaw dropped. "Benson! What are you doing here?"

The short man adjusted his glasses. "Sheriff Tucker said this was the best place to come for the complete story on Rasmus Pierce and his mob. Since I'm our paper's top reporter, here I am."

Justin rubbed a hand along his unshaven jaw. "Couldn't we do this another time? We'd all like to clean up."

"But the town's jumping to hear the facts. The editor's holding the presses for me."

Justin glanced at Constance. "Can you bear up a while longer?"

She nodded. Did he think speaking to a reporter was trying? It wouldn't weary her nearly so much as one more minute of wondering whether Justin would ever trust her again.

Aunt Libby and Mrs. Kelly paid no mind to the reporter. Assured everyone was safe, they took the children under their maternal wings, eager to bathe them and put them safely to bed. Effie launched into her version of their adventure before they'd taken two steps, and Evan broke in with additions and corrections repeatedly before the four were out of earshot.

Chuckling, Alex leaned back against the wagon. "Expect the story as Effie tells it would make a great dime novel."

To Constance's surprise, Justin joined in Alex's chuckle. The angry distance the men had kept between them had evaporated. *What could have happened to change their attitudes so quickly?* she wondered.

The reporter cleared his throat.

At the reminder, Justin lead the small group to the library.

How many scenes the friendly, booklined room had seen in its short existence, Constance thought, lowering herself into a leather chair. Marian and Alexander sat on the couch, Marian's dress a bright splash of blue and gold. The reporter, at Justin's invitation, sat at the desk, while Justin stood beside the fireplace, one arm on the mantle.

Benson pushed up his spectacles. "Let's have the entire story from the beginning."

Marian leaned forward eagerly, her blue eyes outshining the gold buttons on her short jacket. "It all began the day of the train robbery, when Rasmus forced Justin and Constance to marry two days before Justin and I were to wed."

Benson's jaw dangled. "*Forced* them?"

"Marian!"

"Marian!"

Marian just waved a hand to dismiss Constance and Justin.

Constance darted a glance at Justin. His face was dusky with anger and embarrassment.

Marian was continuing blithely, "I guess God arranged that marriage because He knew Justin and Constance were perfect for each other."

Constance kept her gaze glued to her hands, which were clasped tightly in her lap. Still, she knew when Justin moved from the fireplace to stand behind her chair. Awareness of his presence kept her from hearing much of Marian's story.

Justin, Constance, and Alex had little opportunity to tell their own parts in the story, but by the time Marian was through, Constance saw a blessing in Marian's version.

When the reporter finally left, Constance turned to her. "I don't know how to thank you for your generous act. Now the townspeople will know that Justin didn't purposely. . ." She struggled to find a delicate way to state the facts.

Marian grinned. "Leave me standing at the altar?"

Her directness startled Constance. "Uh, that he didn't purposely break your engagement. They'll know that you have forgiven him, and perhaps they will be able to forgive him, too."

Alexander took Marian's elbow. "Something tells me it's the proper time for us to leave. May I see you home, Miss Ames?"

His gaze caught Constance's for a moment. Was it pain she saw in his eyes? "Good-bye, Mrs. Knight." His voice was unexpectedly rough.

The house was incredibly still after they left. Large as it was, it seemed too small now that Aunt Libby and Mrs. Kelly were upstairs putting the children to bed, and Constance and Justin were left alone.

She watched from beneath half-lowered lashes as Justin returned to the fireplace. Unshaven, eyes set in smudges of sleeplessness, wearing his flannel shirt and corduroys, he looked like a stranger to her. Until his eyes met hers, eyes that had so often smiled into hers, had made her feel beautiful and cherished, and horribly guilty. Her gaze skittered away.

Justin picked up the brass poker and pushed idly at the unlit logs that lay always ready for the match.

"How did you talk Rasmus' mother into showing you the hideout?"

It was a moment before she comprehended his question; it was so far from the topic she expected.

"I . . . I think I realized what you have always known. Deceit only bears more evil in its wake. I want to follow the One who is 'the way, the *truth* and the life,' as you do. So I went to Mrs. Pierce with the truth, and hoped that a mother's love would do what was best for her son, and for Effie and Evan."

He put the poker down and crossed the room toward her, his

hands buried in his trouser pockets.

Her breath came faster and shallower. He towered over her, dwarfing what little courage she had. She rose quickly. It would be easier to face him on her feet.

"What you said to Marian just now. . ." He struggled with the words. "Instead of being concerned for yourself, your thought was for me. Thank you."

Had Marian's attitude toward his marriage hurt him? Did he wish it was Marian he was married to now? She kept her gaze averted, afraid to see in his eyes the answer to the question she needed to ask.

"Are you still in love with Marian?"

He settled on the arm of the wing chair. "No. I'm ashamed to say I never loved her as a man should love the woman he marries. When I proposed to her, I didn't know what it meant to love."

He caught her hands and drew her close, pressing his lips to her fingers. "Don't pull your hands away!" He folded them close to his chest. "Last night—was it only last night? It seems a lifetime ago—I was so hurt when I discovered you were an agent, that I didn't think I could ever trust you again.

"Then when Bixby and I went to retrieve the stolen money, he told me that I had been a suspect. That's when I knew everything Marian said about you tonight was true. And I realized what a fool I'd been, raging at what I saw as your deceit and lack of trust. You didn't even know me, it was possible I could be a criminal, yet you moved into my home to protect the children from Rasmus. The trust you gave me is. . .humbling."

"In my heart, I knew you weren't capable of anything so dishonorable as being a partner with Rasmus."

"I said awful things to you last night. It was my pain speaking, but that doesn't excuse me. Can you forgive me?"

She could feel his heart beating beneath the fingers he still held against his flannel-covered chest, and wondered at the knowledge that it beat as erratically as hers. She smiled as she repeated the words he said to her earlier.

"I already have."

He bent his head over her hands.

"I realize the Pinkerton Agency has accomplished much that is good. I admit I don't know how some criminals would ever be brought to justice without the use of deception, though I'd like to think there is a way. I should never have judged you so harshly." He took a deep, shaky breath. "Now that Rasmus has been apprehended, do you plan to return to Chicago and your position as a Pinkerton?"

Was the question as difficult for him as the roughness in his voice indicated?

"That depends. I'd like to fight injustice in the manner a man I know once suggested, by raising children to love our Lord. That is, if. . .if you want me." Her words quivered into a whisper.

"If I want you!" He dropped her hands to wrap her close in his arms. The ardor of his cry drove away her fears and left her lightheaded with joy and relief.

"Are you offering to stay with me because of your marriage vow?"

She nestled her cheek against the soft flannel covering his shoulder, away from his demanding, suddenly possessive eyes.

"I do believe the vows are meant to last forever. But even if I didn't, I should wish to stay." She dared a laughing glance at his face. "Even without the added inducement of the pony and cart Effie suggested."

"You may have any inducement it's within my power to give." His lips pressed against her neck, sending delightful shivers over her. "Mrs. Knight, I've been waiting a lifetime to hear my wife tell me she loves me. Must I wait longer?"

His husky confession compelled her gaze to his. Tears sprang to her eyes until she could no longer see the hunger in his. "I love you, Justi—"

His kiss smothered the words exultantly.

When he finally allowed her to catch her breath, it was to say unsteadily, "I'll spend the rest of our lives trying to show you how much I love you."

The promise was in his eyes as well as his words. It made her feel cherished.

"We didn't thay prayerth, yet."

Constance jerked away from Justin, spinning to face Effie in the same move. "Why aren't you with Aunt Libby and Mrs. Kelly?"

"They fell asleep," Evan offered.

"Yeth."

"Evan, what happened to your hair?"

Effie pulled herself onto the leather seat of a chair. "I cut it."

Evan nodded, mellow light beaming off the uneven, chopped brown hair.

"I wanted it to look like Justin's."

Constance sighed, one hand clutching at the ribbon at her neck. "Oh, my."

Behind her, Justin chuckled. His arms slipped around her waist.

"Something tells me that raising these two will be every bit as challenging as apprehending criminals."

"And every bit as satisfying." She rested the back of her head against his shoulder, smiling at the adorable twins. Contentment slid over her heart. Her family. What a wonderful gift God had given her before she was even willing to acknowledge His existence.

Effie snuggled further into the leather chair.

"Shouldn't we thtart praying? We have lots of people on our litht, you know."

A Letter To Our Readers

Dear Reader:

In order that we might better contribute to your reading enjoyment, we would appreciate your taking a few minutes to respond to the following questions. When completed, please return to the following:

Rebecca Germany, Editor
Heartsong Presents
P.O. Box 719
Uhrichsville, Ohio 44683

1. Did you enjoy reading *An Honest Love*?
   ❑ Very much. I would like to see more books
      by this author!
   ❑ Moderately
      I would have enjoyed it more if _____

   _____

2. Are you a member of *Heartsong Presents*? Yes   No
   If no, where did you purchase this book? _____

   _____

3. What influenced your decision to purchase this
   book? (Check those that apply.)

   ❑ Cover   ❑ Back cover copy

   ❑ Title   ❑ Friends

   ❑ Publicity   ❑ Other _____

4. On a scale from 1 (poor) to 10 (superior), please rate the following elements.

___Heroine   ___Plot

___Hero   ___Inspirational theme

___Setting   ___Secondary characters

5. What settings would you like to see covered in *Heartsong Presents* books?

_____

_____

6. What are some inspirational themes you would like to see treated in future books?_____

_____

_____

7. Would you be interested in reading other *Heartsong Presents* titles?   ❏ Yes   ❏ No

8. Please check your age range:
❏ Under 18   ❏ 18-24   ❏ 25-34
❏ 35-45   ❏ 46-55   ❏ Over 55

9. How many hours per week do you read? _____

Name _____

Occupation _____

Address _____

City _____ State _____ Zip _____

···· Hearts ❤ ng ····

······· Presents ·······

Great Inspirational Romance at a Great Price!

Heartsong Presents books are inspirational romances in contemporary and historical settings, designed to give you an enjoyable, spirit-lifting reading experience. You can choose from 120 wonderfully written titles from some of today's best authors like Colleen L. Reece, Brenda Bancroft, Janelle Jamison, and many others.

When ordering quantities less than twelve, above titles are $2.95 each.

Hearts♥ng Presents
Love Stories Are Rated G!

That's for godly, gratifying, and of course, great! If you love a thrilling love story, but don't appreciate the sordidness of popular paperback romances, **Heartsong Presents** is for you. In fact, **Heartsong Presents** is the *only inspirational romance book club*, the only one featuring love stories where Christian faith is the primary ingredient in a marriage relationship.

Sign up today to receive your first set of four, never before published Christian romances. Send no money now; you will receive a bill with the first shipment. You may cancel at any time without obligation, and if you aren't completely satisfied with any selection, you may return the books for an immediate refund!

Imagine. . .four new romances every month—two historical, two contemporary—with men and women like you who long to meet the one God has chosen as the love of their lives. . .all for the low price of $9.97 postpaid.

To join, simply complete the coupon below and mail to the address provided. **Heartsong Presents** romances are rated G for another reason: They'll arrive *Godspeed!*